Dither Farm

Dither Farm

a novel by **Sid Hite**

Henry Holt and Company
New York

First edition
Published by Henry Holt and Company, Inc.,
115 West 18th Street, New York, New York 10011.
Published simultaneously in Canada by Fitzhenry & Whiteside Ltd.,
91 Granton Drive, Richmond Hill, Ontario L4B 2N5.

Library of Congress Cataloging-in-Publication Data
Hite, Sid.
  Dither Farm : a novel / by Sid Hite
  Summary: A visit by an unusual aunt, a flood, a flying carpet, a kidnapping, and
a groundswell of romance are all part of one summer in the lives of the close-knit
Dither family in southern Virginia.
  ISBN 0-8050-1871-9
  [1. Family life—Fiction. 2. Country life—Fiction. 3. Supernatural—Fiction.
  4. Virginia—Fiction.] I. Title.
PZ7.H64Di 1992
[Fic]—dc20   91-31323

Henry Holt books are available at special discounts
for bulk purchases for sales promotions, premiums,
fund-raising, or educational use. Special editions
or book excerpts can also be created to specification.

Printed in the United States of America
on acid-free paper. ∞

10 9 8 7 6 5 4 3 2 1

For Mildred and Alfred

Laughter released on earth ascends into heaven
and tickles the bottoms of angels' feet.
—*The Comprehensive Guide*

PART ONE

PART ONE

<u>one</u>

IT WAS A HOT, muggy day in Willow County—the hottest so far in an oppressive sequence of hot, muggy weeks. The air lay over the land like a saturated sponge and leaked wetness onto anything that moved. Meteorologists quit measuring humidity with barometric pressure and switched to weighing it by the pound. Old folks sat inside white clapboard houses, listening to whirring window fans harmonize with dehumidifiers groaning in the basement. Many dreamed of moving to Alaska. Farmers stood under shade trees chatting with other farmers. None dared mention the weather; instead they told mechanical troubleshooting stories and regaled each other with jokes. Teenagers commandeered Nora Cook's air-conditioned luncheonette, sipping sodas by the case and keeping the jukebox plied with quarters. Children of various shapes and sizes flocked to the county's preferred swimming holes, where they stirred, splashed, spit, and churned the water into a tepid brown froth. Meanwhile their infant brothers and sisters wallowed in wicker bassinets and attempted to suck coolness from rubber pacifiers. There was no coolness. Leaves drooped from branches, dogs quit chasing cats, and every bullfrog within hopping distance assembled en masse on the dank bottom of Weeping Willow Swamp.

And yet, though it was hot like the Congo and muggy like the Amazon, there were two people in Willow County who did not notice the heat. Their temperatures fluctuated with the flicker of an inner flame. One of these people was sixteen-year-old Clementine Gooden. She sat in a rocking chair on her parents' front porch and watched idly as a few bumblebees buzzed a nearby wisteria bush. She had little to do but wait for two thirty. That was when Henry Dither, the other self-acclimatized person in the county, was in the habit of strolling past the front gate. He was seventeen. When the mantel clock in the living room chimed the half hour, Clementine sighed and twitched her naked toes.

This day marked the twenty-eighth in a row on which Henry Dither appeared at the Gooden gate at exactly two thirty in the afternoon. It was particularly noteworthy because it was the first day upon which he stopped and spoke to Clementine. During the previous month he had been content to wave, mumble, and continue walking as though he had an appointment to keep. But today he stopped.

His timing was more important than he would ever know. That very morning Clementine had decided that a month of waving and mumbling was a sufficient period of preliminary gesturing, and now it was time for real courtship. She reasoned, "Okay, already. That's one cycle of the moon. I don't mind a bashful guy, but if he's too shy to run the risk of flirting, then . . . well, I'm going to start sitting on the *back* porch at two thirty."

As Henry breasted the hill overlooking the Gooden property and saw the house below, he paused to spit in his hand and pat the cowlick cresting his head. He wiped his palms on the seat of his jeans, checked to see if his zipper was up, then tucked in his shirt before resuming his approach. Clementine sensed his arrival before seeing him. In a slow, controlled manner she turned her gaze to the front gate. Henry was standing by it with his shoulders hunched and his hands poked deep in his hip pockets. His attention was focused directly on her, and it was obvious he had something to say. She watched and waited. It took him a few moments to build up his voice. He shuddered once, rocked back on his heels, then swallowed air. Clementine cocked an ear as he pursed his lips to speak. But he did not speak. Instead he stifled a hiccup and turned red. There ensued another lengthy pause, after which he coughed nervously and called: "Hi. How are you doing today?"

"Finally I hear you speak," Clementine snickered.

"What?" Henry cupped a hand to his ear.

"I said I'm fine this week."

"Oh . . . great . . . me too."

There was another pause, during which Henry slapped a fly that had settled on his neck. He flicked it to the ground and continued. "Say, Clementine, I was wondering if you'd come here to the gate and have a conversation."

"Now, Henry?" she inquired. "Or next week sometime?"

"Now." Henry nodded.

Clementine leaned forward in the rocker and rested her elbows on the porch rail. "Henry, don't you think it's odd that this is the first time you've spoken to me all summer?"

"Odd?"

"Yes, odd."

"I said hi a couple of times."

"You said hi. I never heard you." Clementine scowled.

Henry kicked at the dirt. "Clementine, are you coming to the gate or not?"

"Hold your britches. I'm coming."

The sight of Clementine rising from the rocker, moving along the porch, descending the steps, and then crossing the front yard had a profound and disturbing effect on the young suitor. His stomach turned a half gainer, and he could hear what sounded like the Atlantic Ocean crashing upon its sandy shores. (An astonishing feat, considering the ocean is more than a hundred miles east of Willow County.) For the first time in a month he felt the wet heaviness of the weather.

Clementine wore a blue cotton dress upon which she had embroidered a chain of wildflowers. Not quite knee length, it fit snugly to her nubile form. Her coal-black hair cascaded past her round shoulders in a rush of curls and bounced to a general conclusion midway down her back. The dark locks framed her pretty face in movement and complemented her peachy-cream complexion. Her hazel-green eyes shimmered in the sunlight like emeralds, her lips sparkled like polished apple skins, and her teeth gleamed like fine china. Her pert nose fit perfectly between her forehead and her small chin. Beneath that chin Henry saw what he had been hoping to see—the yellow hint of a buttercup.

Leopold Hillacre could have floated overhead in a hot-air balloon and Henry never would have noticed.

Henry had a difficult time maintaining his composure. When he began to speak, his voice rose and fell irregularly, and words exited his mouth in confused clusters. It was impossible for Clementine to follow what he was saying. Indeed, she had to exercise her imagination to understand him at all. Yet somehow she managed to collect his fragmentary quips, provide them with a context, and respond as though their conversation made perfect sense. For the eight minutes they stood by the gate talking, she drew clarity from chaos, intent from innuendo, and meaning from obscurity. And not only was she understanding, she also exhibited foresight. She proposed that they meet the following day and go to Nora Cook's for a milk shake.

Henry walked away from the Gooden property in a beatific daze.

In an effort to express his immense joy, he composed a couplet, which he muttered over and over: "Clementine Gooden, sweeter than pumpkin puddin'. Clementine Gooden, sweeter than pumpkin pie." The words were like a marching chant. They carried him blissfully along, step after step, until eventually he looked up and realized he had walked halfway to Binkerton. That he could amble so far without noticing was final proof that he was in love.

That evening the extended spell of hot, muggy weather dissipated in the face of a cool breeze filtering down from the north. You could hear a sigh of relief rising over Willow County as beleaguered residents rushed out of doors to greet the fresh air. Those who owned front porches utilized them in the proper manner. The world had returned to a tolerable state. Moods long dour were uplifted, and many people were inspired to atone for their sins. Children voluntarily confessed to petty crimes of the past, husbands and wives told their spouses whatever they wanted to hear, and siblings suddenly forgave each other for previous slights. Dogs chased cats with renewed vigor, cows resumed mooing, and a caucus of bullfrogs emerged from Weeping Willow Swamp croaking the Hallelujah Chorus.

"I'm not hungry tonight," Clementine informed her mother when she was called to supper. She remained in her favorite rocker with her feet propped up on the porch rail. Her mind was a million miles away. She stared upward and outward, watching as darkness enveloped the land and a zillion stars filled the sky. Her vision, enhanced by a soaring spirit, seemed to extend forever. She noticed a small star set off from the others. It appeared to throb and twinkle with particularly earnest intent. After studying it awhile, she named it Henry.

Henry Dither, at that moment, was a mile and a half away, standing in the bathroom of his parents' house. He too had skipped supper, but his thoughts were less lofty than Clementine's. His thoughts were focused on an object near to hand. Staring at him in the mirror was the meanest, most tenacious cowlick in the state of Virginia, and he had challenged it to a showdown. "Either you or me," he threatened the formidable opponent with a pair of scissors. The cowlick laughed. It had thrived for seventeen years and saw no reason to die now. In the past, Henry had tried to tame it with mounds of petroleum jelly. Once he had painted it with nail polish and worn a bathing cap for half an hour. But each time the cowlick had slept only a moment before reawakening. Now things were different—Henry was in love and he would not be defeated. He flattened the opened scissors against his head and snapped the handle shut. The cowlick was no match for blades of steel. It went limp and fell to the floor. For good measure Henry stomped on the disembodied tuft, then gathered it up and flushed it down the toilet. With mixed feelings he watched his old nemesis swirl out of sight. On the one hand he was glad to see it go. On the other he regretted the bald spot.

At two thirty the following afternoon, when Henry emerged from the woods and approached the Gooden gate, he was delighted to see Clementine waiting for him in a splash of bright colors. She wore a pink blouse tucked neatly into blue shorts. A red ribbon held back her curls, and the green tennis shoes on her feet were laced with bright yellow strings.

"I've never seen you wear a hat," she greeted her caller.

"Oh, this?" He reached up. "I wear it sometimes."

"It's sporty."

"Glad you like it. Are you ready? Let's go." Henry tipped his cap and started walking.

It was just over a mile from the Goodens' front gate to the entrance into Nora Cook's luncheonette. It was an awkward walk for Henry. He felt relaxed inside, but he said things like: "I was wondering a darn flower if you?" and "Yesterday when they grow by the creek. How did you, just nevermind?" and "Fine here. Find we hope an empty booth."

They did find an empty booth. Henry made a beeline for it and sat down. Then he remembered his manners and jumped up. His knee accidentally hit the table and sent a sugar bowl sailing toward the floor. He swooped to catch it with his cap, but just as he did, he remembered the bald spot. His reaction was swift. He slapped the cap back on his head, shattering the china bowl. Sugar poured over his shoulders and dropped to the floor.

"Not bad for openers," Clementine laughed. "Do that often?"

"Not lately." Henry was embarrassed, but he couldn't deny the humor in the situation. He grinned at his date. "I break sugar bowls only on special occasions."

"Is this a special occasion?" Clementine asked as she sat down across from him in the booth.

"Sure is. Here I am with the prettiest girl in the whole of Willow County—I do think you're prettier than Millie Ross, no matter what others say—and we came together on a date. As far as I'm concerned, that's special."

"You do have a way with words." Clementine smiled.

"Takes me a while to get warmed up," Henry admitted.

"Me too," she said. "Tell me more."

Time is an abundant commodity in Willow County. The supply greatly exceeds the demand. Consequently the inhabitants of this rural domain are rarely, if ever, in a hurry to get anywhere or do anything. Only a few of them have even heard of the rat race, and none comprehend its power. For Willowites it is an urban myth. (There are a few old-timers who remember Abe Maddy and his forty-foot-long, oval, wooden, six-lane rat track, which he kept in his barn. He also kept a stable of trained racers, which he would fit with leather harnesses attached to small, two-wheel carts with numbers painted on the sides. Cubes of Muenster cheese were loaded onto the carts as the rats lined up at the starting gate. The first one to cross the finish line got to eat the cheese in his cart. They were fierce competitors. Betting was widespread.) Willowites suffer a distinctly rural threat. Rather than stress from a lack of time, they must guard themselves against tranquility fatigue and other pitfalls of time wealth. Lethargy is an active force in Willow. Snoozes, naps, and siestas are limited to two or three hours a day, coffee is offered in every household, and vigorous sporting games are encouraged. A mother's greatest fear is having a child come down with the dreaded Rip Van Winkle syndrome.

The pace and atmosphere of the place is so generally relaxed that many etymologists believe the expression "If it ain't broke, don't fix it" has its roots in the hills and valleys of Willow County. Other linguists attribute to Willow the saying "Don't do today what can be done tomorrow." Both groups have the sentiment correct, but their epigrammatic phrasing is incorrect. The expression most favored by indigenous Willowites is "Rushing a foredrawn conclusion is like shooting a dead skunk: You just make a lot of noise and waste a lot of buckshot."

And so time crawls forward in Willow County. After their first date in Nora Cook's luncheonette, Clementine and Henry began to see each other on a regular basis. As the weeks passed, they earned the reputation of a couple. When not in their regular booth at Nora's, they were often exploring the green fields and forests of the countryside. It was there, in the privacy of nature, that they felt most comfortable investigating the depths of their involvement. It soon developed into one of those relationships that is generally called a romance. Romances, as many know, often lead to kissing. This one did. And with the kissing came an increase in passion for their investigations. It was a romance that grew in the same manner that teenagers grow: in awkward fits and spurts. But they adapted, and made rules where rules were necessary. Frequently they rendezvoused by a creek in an apple orchard, where they would lie long hours listening to the seductive babble of water rushing over rocks. Twice (it was rumored) they went skinny-dipping in the rock quarry.

In time . . . well, they had their moments.

two

BENEFITING FROM THE casual pace and excess tranquility in Willow County, the romance between Clementine and Henry bloomed and flourished for two years without a major misunderstanding. Time, so to speak, was on their side. But time, at whatever rate it passes, does nothing if it does not bring change. Henry suddenly realized this on the fifth of June, in his nineteenth year of life, when Clementine was in the act of graduating from Willow High.

Henry had graduated the previous June, and that evening as he sat in the familiar assembly hall and observed the familiar faces in the crowd, his mind began to harbor alien thoughts. They were tricky thoughts that turned on him and ate at his equanimity. In three days Clementine was scheduled to leave Willow County to visit an elderly aunt in Iceland. Henry feared the worst. "I must be missing something," he reflected. "She is going to Iceland to visit some old lady she doesn't even know, for seven weeks, and no one is making her do it. Isn't that what women do when they are preparing to leave their lovers?" He suddenly imagined a tall, fair-haired Viking waiting for Clementine at the airport. He gasped, "How could I be so blind?" Love's lasso tightened at his throat, and his chest began to constrict. He felt like there was no longer enough oxygen available for him in the stuffy auditorium.

A hush fell over the crowd as Henry rose abruptly from his seat. Millie Ross was speaking at the podium, and she paused to see what he was doing. When she paused, all eyes followed hers and set upon Henry. He feigned nonchalance and began to work his way through the crowd. It was a disastrous trip. Halfway to the aisle, he kicked over Flea Jenfries's purse. Keys, coins, and candy spilled loudly onto the concrete floor. Henry's concentration was jarred long enough for him to step on Willard Gardner's foot. Willard, shocked with sudden pain, wailed like the six-year-old he was. The audience turned from curious to hostile as Henry hurried toward the exit. Clementine observed all this from the stage. To say she was bewildered is putting it mildly. Henry turned at the outer doors and stared in her direction. She winced and clutched her diploma. Millie Ross, never one to share the spotlight, waited until he was out of the building before continuing her valedictorian speech.

Henry lay low for the next few days, camping in a duck blind near Weeping Willow Swamp. He understood that his fears were irrational. He knew Clementine would not mess around without telling him. He accepted that he had acted like a fool. Logic told him to go to her with apologies. Yet logic is a weak thing when pitted against a wounded heart. By the time his rational powers had won control over his emotions, he was so embarrassed, he decided to remain hidden. When his best friend Garland Barlow found him and delivered the news that Willard Gardner had a broken toe, it did little to lift his sagging spirits.

Clementine had no idea what had happened to Henry. She still had not heard from him as she rode with her father, Talbert Gooden, to the airport in Bricksburg. She instructed him to drop her at the entrance to the terminal. She was hoping Henry would be there to say good-bye. He was, but since she did not enter the men's restroom, she was unaware of his presence. She checked her suitcase at the ticket counter, then wandered through the airport for thirty minutes. Her thoughts ran between excitement over her pending trip and disappointment over Henry. Where was he? Why had he not come to the graduation party? How come he was not there to wish her farewell? And where in the hell had he been hiding for three days?

The minutes ticked by with Henry failing to materialize. Finally Clementine's boarding announcement rattled the overhead loud-speakers. She approached the gate and handed the woman her tick-et. Before walking away, she threw a last, doubtful glance behind her. Something was dashing through the crowd. Henry skidded to a halt. Clementine did not know whether to slug him or hug him. "Where have you been?" she demanded.

"I don't know," he puffed. "I just came to tell you to have a good time in Iceland. I'm sorry I'm an idiot."

"You're not an idiot, but your timing is awful. I can't talk. I've got a plane to catch."

"I know. Get on it." Henry pointed toward the tarmac.

She hesitated. "I've never flown."

"It's easy. Just sit there and hold your breath," Henry said reas-suringly. "I suppose you know you'll be missed."

"I hope so." Clementine stepped forward to plant a parting kiss on Henry's lips. It was bestowed with the accuracy of a lover. She turned. "Behave yourself," she instructed as she stepped into the connecting corridor.

"Me?" Henry said, but she was already gone.

Clementine sat in seat 17A, a window seat in the smoking section. Although she was not a smoker, she carried a single cigarette, which she planned to light somewhere over the Atlantic. She was not sure why. Her elbows dug into the armrests as the jet thrust into the sky. It was a strange feeling . . . to be flying from Bricksburg, Virginia, to Reykjavík, Iceland. She knew almost nothing about her aunt Emma Bean. The invitation to visit had been the first contact anyone in the Gooden clan had had with her for fifteen years. She was Clementine's great-aunt on her mother's side. As a teenager she had shocked her family by running away from home and traveling all over the world. No one could remember her exact age, but she had to be at least sixty-five. Perhaps closer to seventy.

Here are the facts Clementine had managed to compile. Emma Alderson Bean: never married, studied at a university in Denmark, did research in parapsychology, worked frequently as a consultant to the U.S. government. Her house was situated on an isolated cove in a bay near a volcano in Iceland. She continued to travel, was an amateur biologist, once killed a man; had auburn hair, sang, played piano, and collected oriental carpets. The few people in Willow County who had actually met Emma described her as a feisty beauty with a rich, contralto voice. It was said she had more personality than was necessary for three people.

According to the story Clementine had heard as a child, the man Emma Bean killed was a guide from a remote village in Tibet. He was a dubious fellow with one eye whom Emma had hired while trekking from Katmandu, Nepal, to Tsaparang, Tibet, in 1943. During much of the journey she had traveled alone, but she decided she needed a guide to lead her through a particularly formidable mountain range near Lhasa. The one-eyed man led her along a twisting, narrow trail, and then, at a precipice overhanging a rocky ravine, informed her that he was a professional thief. He demanded money, pointing a derringer at her to emphasize his meaning. (Emma's Tibetan was spotty, but she understood the gun.) Emma realized the desperado planned to kill her after she handed over the dough. She indicated to him that he could have her money, but it was in a pouch strapped around her stomach. If he would honor her modesty and turn his back for a moment, she gesticulated, then she would undress and fetch him the pouch. For effect, Emma pretended to blush. The bandit considered a moment, then complied with her request. As soon as he turned his back, she swiftly and squarely kicked him in the buttocks, propelling him to a gory death on the rocky valley floor below. Even as a child, Clementine understood it was a necessary act of survival.

Clementine put her face against the window and looked down at the wispy altocumulus clouds. Through the patches of white fluff she could see the dark surface of the Atlantic Ocean. It amazed her that she was actually flying and would soon land in Reykjavík. Just a few hours, she counted, and she would be face to face with the mysterious old aunt. Little did she know what to expect, nor could she imagine how they would occupy themselves for seven weeks. After a long sigh, she reached for the cigarette in her purse.

Henry behaved in a relatively normal manner for the first week or so after Clementine's departure. By day he helped his father on the farm, and in the evenings he rode his bicycle to the river and fished for bass. He checked *The Pickwick Papers* out of the library and read at least one chapter every night. Other than the scraggly beard that sprouted on his face, there was no warning that he was about to go off the deep end.

It happened swiftly, on a Saturday morning after he awoke from a night of troubling dreams. Initially he suffered nothing worse than an attitude problem, but it grew steadily, and by midafternoon, when he hooked up with Marvin Jinks, he was on the verge of a breakdown. Marvin took him to the Hot Spot in Binkerton. After a short time in the dimly lit, smoke-filled parlor, Henry grew restless and decided to challenge the world.

The Hot Spot had seen his kind before. He never had a chance. He hit the pavement with a thump.

The next morning he woke up in the rear of a Greyhound bus parked in the Port Authority terminal in midtown Manhattan. Marvin Jinks was tugging at his sleeve.

"Get with it, Henry. We're here already."

"I can't believe I let you talk me into this," Henry moaned.

"What was I supposed to do, take you home looking like an accident? Relax, Henry. This is New York City. We're gonna see some things you never even thought of before."

"La dee da." Henry rose and stretched his sore muscles.

Some things he'd never thought of, yes, but Henry's heart was not into the thrill of it. He did not particularly mind sleeping in Central Park, and he liked some of the homeless friends he made, but the constant honking and pronounced lack of space made him nervous. After three days he called it quits.

"What the hell's the matter with you?" Marvin asked.

"Nothing. I just want to go home while I still have enough money for a bus ticket."

Marvin tried to reason with him. "Ya gotta give the place a chance. There're more opportunities here in one day than there are in a lifetime in Willow County. What are you going to do there?"

"Take it easy, fish . . . I don't know." Henry shrugged.

"You'll be bored in less than a week."

"I'd rather be bored than bothered."

"Then go back." Marvin looked disgusted. "Go back and marry Clementine, and settle down like a good boy."

"Not a bad idea." Henry smiled before walking away.

Henry got off the bus at Aylor's Store and went inside for a soda. When Jimmy saw him, he shook his head doubtfully and remarked, "It isn't easy being a bachelor. I think you better mosey on home and get some rest."

Suddenly, it seemed to Henry, he did feel exhausted. He forgot about wanting a soda and turned on his heels for home. Once there, securely ensconced in his own bed, he proceeded to sleep for two days and a night. Yet rather than restore his spirits, the sleep sank him further into a funk. When he eventually crawled out of bed, a shadow hovered over him that even the sun could not dispel. His mother encountered him in the kitchen. She did not hesitate in shooing him out of the house. "You can return when you're human again," she said.

Henry continued on a downhill course. He set up camp on the back side of Leopold Hillacre's property and avoided all contact with people. He passed much of his time reading thick, erudite books borrowed from Leopold's library. They were books he did not understand; they only confused and depressed him. He considered training to be an intellectual. He compiled a list of important words and practiced pronouncing them in his tent at night. Soon, armed with an increased vocabulary, he started to analyze life and think like a philosopher. What was worse, he began to write poems. One of them, entitled "If I Had Thou Now," ran for sixty pages. Even he could not bear to read it when it was done.

Meanwhile, in Iceland, Clementine felt like she had been eating encyclopedias. From the moment Aunt Emma Bean—dressed in a flashy jumpsuit and wearing a felt fedora—met her at the airport in Reykjavík to the present evening on the porch overlooking the bay, Clementine stayed busy absorbing an endless infusion of life's facts and theories. New worlds that she had never imagined were suddenly presented whole before her eyes. The details were abundant. She had only to ask a question and Emma Bean would reply with a thorough, insightful dissertation that any college professor would proudly claim. And on any subject. It was as though Emma knew something about everything. Clementine could not judge if all of what she heard was scientifically accurate, but it sounded true, and she was veritably impressed.

For example: This evening Clementine had nodded toward a

18

large volcano looming beyond the bay and remarked, "I bet the sky will really light up when that one blows." Her comment elicited a response that included the names of every significant volcano on the planet, past and present. She heard secondhand accounts of lava walking in the Pahoa region of Hawaii and firsthand tales of expeditions into the Krafla Caldera region of Iceland. She heard of the Moduhardini, caused by the Fires of Skafta, and learned what fluorine does to sheep in the fields. She was told of the peculiarities of the North American Plate, and was apprised of the latest geophysical predictions. Soon she knew more about volcanic hot spots than most people know about their noses.

It was near the end of Clementine's visit, and as the two women sat in wicker rocking chairs admiring the view across the bay, Emma held in her lap the frayed end of an antique oriental carpet. The remainder of the rug was rolled over her legs, extending to the floor. With nimble, dextrous fingers she darned a badly worn corner with silk thread. At the same time she gave Clementine a little room to speak. While they chatted, the setting sun emblazoned the western sky with magnificent colors.

"Aunt Emma," Clementine ended a quiet lull. "I've had such a wonderful visit. I'm so glad I got a chance to get to know you. Thank you for your hospitality."

"You have been a perfect guest."

"It's hard to believe that seven weeks have flown by so fast. It seems like I arrived just yesterday."

Emma chuckled softly.

"I hope someday you will find a way to visit Willow County. I know the Gooden side of the family would be pleased to see you." As Clementine said these words, she looked at Emma and wondered about her age. Emma was still a very attractive woman. There was no gray in her thick auburn hair, and the few lines in her face moved upward with character. Her hands controlled the needle with expert steadiness, and she did not squint her eyes as she made the delicate repairs. Clementine had to ask, "Aunt Emma, how do you stay so young?"

Emma's reply was uncharacteristically brief. "Simple. I think young."

"You think young?" Clementine said doubtfully.

"Yep. Think young and you are young." Emma grinned. "Nothing profound about it." Emma reached for her teacup and snorted in the manner of a laugh.

"Oh," said Clementine. She had the distinct feeling that Emma was keeping something from her.

Emma changed the subject. "So you'll be going to college this fall?"

"I'm not sure. I've been accepted. It depends . . . well, it depends on several things." Clementine blushed with confusion.

"Oh, and are the several things wrapped up in a package named Henry? He sounds nice, from what little you've told me."

"He is . . . nice." Clementine paused to reflect. "He's more than nice. I just . . . well, I guess I'm not sure."

"You'll be sure soon enough," Emma said confidently.

A few days later, as Clementine sat in seat 23C on the flight home to Virginia, she made two entries in her journal.

The first: "Time is less abundant in Iceland than it is in Willow County."

The second: "My entire visit seems to have taken place over a single, bottomless cup of herbal tea. Was I put under a spell? Or maybe hypnotized?" This was a question that would haunt her for years; a question that she would never properly resolve.

She closed her journal and peered anxiously out the window at the bright blue sky. In the span of five more hours, she would be home again, in the green, tranquil world of Willow County.

20

three

CLEMENTINE WAS MET at the airport by her mother Pat, her little sister Molly, and her good friend Flea Jenfries. After a boisterous reception the women exited the terminal and loaded into Flea's blue station wagon. Almost immediately after settling in the car, Clementine sensed that something was wrong. Her mother sat quietly in the front seat with her arms crossed and her eyes set upon the farmland passing on the right. When she spoke, she did so curtly, in a perfunctory tone. Molly was silent. Clementine figured her sister must be under gag orders. Flea's eyes were on the road, though she at least had the courtesy to ask a question or two about Iceland. Finally, after twenty minutes of awkward silence, just as they drove by Aylor's Store, Clementine forced the issue. "Did someone die?"

"No," said Pat.

"Then why the zipped lips?"

"You'll find out soon enough," Pat answered.

Clementine guessed. "Something has happened to Henry."

"He's . . . changed," said Pat.

"What do you mean by that?" Clementine asked.

"Gone bonkers," interjected Molly.

"Just changed," explained Pat.

Henry Dither was barefoot and shirtless as he squatted in shallow water under a bridge spanning the Mattaponi River. He held a can with holes punched in the sides. His concentration was focused downward, into the water. Consequently he did not see Garland Barlow approach, and was startled by the deep voice: "What are you, a troll?"

"I'm scooping minnows," Henry snapped at his friend.

"Had any luck?"

"About a dozen."

"I reckon I can use them," Garland said matter-of-factly.

"Garland, why would I want to give you the minnows I've been breaking my back to catch?" Henry asked without looking up.

"Oh, because Clementine Gooden got home this afternoon, and I don't figure you're gonna be fishing this evening."

Henry looked at Garland, looked in the bucket beside him, and grinned. "You're welcome to the minnows, Garland, but I've caught only three so far."

Dot Dither laughed when she saw her son enter the house. "Tired of living in a tent?" she asked.

"I came home to apologize to you, Mom. And to shave." Henry kissed his mother's cheek before bounding upstairs to the bathroom. After a moment he called down, "Is Dad very mad?"

Dot chuckled and called back, "You know Sherwood."

Clementine was waiting at the gate when Henry came over the hill. She ran her fingers through her hair, dipped her head to the side, and looked at him questioningly.

"Hi, Clementine. Have a good trip?" Henry asked.

"It was exciting. I saw a volcano smoking."

"You world traveler, you."

"So . . . what did you do all summer?"

"Not much. Next to nothing."

"Nothing?" She put her hands on her hips.

"Oh, I fished and farted around. Camped out some. That sort of thing. Mostly though I . . . well, I kinda missed you."

She softened her stance. "How much kinda?"

"Kinda a lot," Henry admitted. "Actually, like crazy."

"Come here," she said, but it was she who stepped forward.

Less than a year later, during the Fourth of July Binkerton Independence Festival, Henry took Clementine to a dance benefit for the Willow County Volunteer Fire Department. Tickets were ten dollars a head. The Hunkerdowns had been hired for the job. They played an eclectic mixture of bluegrass, pop, and soul. Except for the occasional squeal of microphone feedback, they sounded nearly professional. Henry waited until they took a break to wet their whistles, then ushered Clementine outside to a dimly lit picnic area. He coughed nervously, cast several furtive looks into the shadows, then fell to his knees. "Clementine, give me your hand."

"Are you stuck?" she asked with a grin.

"No, I'm not stuck."

"Then why do you want my hand?"

"I want to marry it," Henry blurted. "And you, too. I want to marry everything about you."

"Well, well. I was wondering if it would come to this."

"Does that mean yes?"

"It means I'll think about it."

"Think about it!" Henry jumped up. "Give me a hint."

"Come here," she said, and then—lips being instruments of clairvoyance—Henry had the hint he was hoping for.

They were married the following May, on a green and glorious Saturday afternoon. Songbirds were singing, and wildflowers were busy luring pollinators. The ceremony was held on a grassy knoll, high on the highest hill in Willow County. It was a spot long associated with propitious events. It afforded a commanding view of the fields and forests below. One could look down and watch as the sluggish Mattaponi River looped aimlessly across the land, or peer out to where distant hills diminished in soft lumps along the horizon.

The Hunkerdowns set up by a tree near the clearing and serenaded the arriving guests with gospel tunes. As the masses gained the open area on the summit, they greeted one another in merry voices, waved multicolored handkerchiefs, tipped broad-brimmed hats, winked, whistled, nodded, and smiled.

"Ah, the carnival of life," Jimmy Aylor said to Leopold Hillacre, who was walking just ahead.

"How I love a nuptial affair," adjoined Leopold. "It stirs the blood and sharpens the senses."

"Indeed. And if the wedding doesn't stir your blood," Jimmy puffed, "this hill certainly will."

"Some of us are in better shape than others," observed the elderly yet spry Leopold.

The well-wishers mingled in the clearing and socialized until the Reverend John Clarence Rowe strode from the woods and approached the makeshift altar. "Hup," he called, reducing the din of chitchat to a murmur. Everyone rushed to take their places. After an ecclesiastical pause, the Reverend turned his palms upward. It was a signal for the betrothed to approach. Henry preceded Clementine up the grassy lane. He looked handsome in his rented tuxedo and would have qualified for dapper had he not fidgeted constantly. His fiancée was a contrast in composure. As Clementine glided forth in a white not-quite-calf-length gown, an appreciable "ah" arose from the crowd. She was stunning—the epitome of a beaming bride. The women envied her grace. The men envied Henry.

J. C. Rowe began the service with a traditional talk on society and the importance of maintaining holy institutions. He spoke of family, commitment, the profundity of love, and the concept of heavenly bliss. Nothing new, and yet his words worked magic on some of the more sensitive guests.

Flea Jenfries was the first to display her feelings. She sniffled and made snorting noises into her handkerchief. Next Missy Hobkins began to exhale long, roller-coaster sighs that ended in high-pitched squeaks. Once Flea and Missy got going, they were joined by Bellamonte Smoot, who made a sound best described as a combination sob and honk. Meanwhile Pat Gooden began to wheeze and Dot Dither started gasping for air. Then, as if on cue, Willa Tucker voiced an emotional outpouring that seemed to combine all of the aforementioned histrionics. It was not long before she was shaking in her seat. The guests sitting nearby were uncertain whether to ignore her or send for help.

Perhaps due to the outbreak over the prologue, the Reverend Rowe cut the ceremonial vows to the bone. (Somebody said it was because he was late for a bowling tournament in Binkerton.) He put his hand on Henry's shoulder and asked: "Do you promise to stand by Clementine no matter what happens?"

"I do."

"Clementine, will you care for Henry always?"

"I will."

"Do you love each other?"

"Yes."

"Any objections?" The Reverend scanned the congregation. When no one replied, he announced, "Exchange rings and then kiss so all can see. You are married before these witnesses."

As bride and groom locked lips, a hoot escaped from a band of bachelors standing in the back. It was followed by a holler, and the reception informally began. It was a spirited affair that continued long after the newlyweds had picked rice from their hair and departed on their honeymoon. Besides inventing several new dance steps, the revelers managed to rid the world of thirty-two pies, seven hundred ham biscuits, five platters of vegetables, two blocks of cheese, twenty gallons of cider, eight vats of coffee, three jugs of applejack, and innumerable mints, gumdrops, and jellybeans.

Earlier, before Clementine and Henry left the knoll to go on their honeymoon, an event occurred that would shape profoundly the future of their lives. Pat Gooden approached and handed them a telegram that had arrived that morning. It was sent from Iceland. Clementine read it first and was rendered speechless by its contents. She was shaking when she handed it to Henry. He too was at a loss for words.

"Congratulations stop," it said. "Sorry could not be there stop. In honor of this fine day I deed you my farm near Aylor's Store stop. I do not need it stop. Since I am not there you cannot argue stop. Lots of love Emma Bean."

Clementine and Henry honeymooned in the Shenandoah Valley. They stayed a week, in a room with a heart-shaped bed. It rained every day. They hardly noticed.

After the honeymoon was over, they returned to Willow County and went straight to work on their seventy-five-acre farm. During their first several months of occupancy, they scrubbed and painted the interior of the house, scraped and painted the exterior, planted a garden, constructed a chicken coop, dug a root cellar, mended fences, fixed gates, and put a sign at the end of their long dirt driveway. It read: DITHER FARM.

They were understandably proud. The house, built before the Civil War, had twelve rooms. It was dry and handsome, situated on a soft slope facing south. Running from the front porch to the creek bisecting the yard was a stone sidewalk. Thirty-eight acres of the farm was in field, the soil having a long history of nitrogen-fixing legumes. It had lain fallow for years and was now prime for the plow. There was a small apple orchard on the ridge behind the barn. Beyond that lay a two-acre pond surrounded by tall pines. Abutting the pines was a forest of mixed hardwoods. The property extended into the floodplains of the Mattaponi.

One hot, muggy day after the Dithers had been living on the farm for a couple of months, Henry cleared the weeds away from the back of the barn and pried open a door that had been shut for years. His eyes adjusted slowly as indirect light crept into the corners of the dank basement. He sneezed as moldy air rushed past him and evaporated in the heat.

At first all he could see were cobwebs and planks of rotting lumber. Then he noticed an object in the middle of the dark basement. It was partially obscured by a tarp. Henry stood framed in the door and eyed the thing with growing bafflement, until curiosity carted him forward to where he removed the tarp. At a glance he could not say what he had just uncovered. It was obviously a large, mechanical contraption, but for what purpose he did not know. The longer he studied it, the more confused he became. Initially he recognized it as a commercial sausage grinder. Then he realized it was an industrial cheese processor. Next he perceived that it was a prototype for a grist mill. Or perhaps a taffy maker.

Actually he had no idea what it was until Clementine poked her head through the open door, squinted her eyes, then exclaimed, "I've always wanted a cider press! Now we know what to do with our apples."

"I was just thinking the same thing, honey."

*   *   *

By late November of that year, "Clementine's Cider" had met with popular approval in three counties. The Dithers had more orders than they could fill. (Their special blend was prized as stock for the hard stuff.) They went up on their price per gallon, hoping the move would ease demand. It did not; it merely brought in more profits. They were forced to expand the business by purchasing apples from other orchards and setting up a distributorship. At the same time they were harvesting cash from the cider business, Henry arranged to have some hardwoods select-cut from the back side of the farm. He caught the market at a premium and received a large payment. Suddenly, it seemed to them, without actually trying they had accumulated a sizable nest egg. It was the source of much pride and many late-night discussions. They kept it in a box under the bed.

"Part of me wants to crack our egg and use it to travel around the world," Clementine mused one night. "We could fly to Iceland and stay with Aunt Emma for a while."

"Her again," Henry mumbled in a reserved tone.

"It would be interesting."

Henry propped himself on an elbow and turned in bed to look at Clementine. "The egg is half yours. Iceland doesn't appeal to me, but I'll consider anything for you."

"Only part of me wants to travel." Clementine nestled close to her husband. "The rest wants to stay here and start a family."

"Like I said," Henry grinned in the dark, "I'll consider any proposal you make."

The following spring they cracked the nest egg and acquired various articles for the farm. Mostly they were practical expenditures. A portion of the money went as a down payment on a Farmall B tractor. Another portion went for seed and fertilizer. Some of it bought domestic items. A bit went for furniture and clothes. The remainder they saved for a rainy day, except for the twelve dollars Henry spent on a box of cigars when he learned Clementine was pregnant.

"Hey, have a cigar," he hailed every friend he met.

"What's the occasion, Henry?"

"Clementine and I are pregnant."

"Well, congratulations. But aren't cigars usually given out *after* the child is born?"

"I don't know. I'm new at this. Do you want one or not?"

PART TWO

four

TIME MAY BE MEASURED in minutes or millennia, seconds or centuries. Although there is much of the stuff in Willow County, it nevertheless does move forward and eventually come to pass. Like everywhere in the world, the years add up.

Over a dozen of them have accumulated since the glorious birth of the Dithers' first child, Holly. Clementine still laughs when she is reminded of how oddly Henry behaved that year. She saved as a memento the cigar box he brought home from Aylor's Store. The cardboard container originally held twenty-five Panatella DeLuxes. It now holds baby curls and beadwork identity bracelets from the maternity ward at Hilltop Memorial Hospital. Currently there are four bracelets in the box: two itsy-bitsy pink ones and two itty-bitty blue ones. Henry has transformed as an individual since the first snippets of Holly's hair were labeled and put away. After he saw that Clementine did not break or fall apart easily, he began to adjust to the role of being a father. With each subsequent birth he became mellower and mellower. By the time Archibald (number four) arrived, Henry was so relaxed, he actually got an hour of sleep the night before the little fellow was born.

Clementine and Henry sat on the front porch holding hands and watching the sun set. The children were inside playing cards on the kitchen table. Earlier, a thunderstorm had rolled over the farm and driven them all indoors. Hidden in the reeds along the creek, a bullfrog croaked for his friends to come out and play. Clementine rested her head on Henry's shoulder and laughed her laugh she reserved for special occasions. Henry knew it well. "Don't tell me," he said. "You have news."

"I do." She giggled.

"And is this news the sort that will require us to start thinking of names we might use?" Henry asked.

"It is." She giggled again.

There was a pause during which Henry scratched the stubble on his face. Then he avowed, "I'll be wibberniffled."

"You'll be what? Wibnerfelled?"

"Wibberniffled," he corrected his wife. "It means living in a dream with the one you love. You give me that feeling so often, I thought up a word to express it."

"Henry," Clementine said, "you're a genius."

"Thank you, darling. I think five is a perfect number."

"It's perfect for kids."

Together they watched the sun drop below the horizon and the faint twinkle of many stars appear in the sky. In that crepuscular moment, as day was becoming night, a wild goose flew south along the creek and passed directly in front of the house. It was a gander. It honked when it went by. In the silence left behind, Clementine applied pressure to her husband's hand and observed, "I'm starting to feel a little wibberniffled myself."

*　　　*　　　*

Meanwhile the card game in the kitchen was starting to unravel. "Got any sevens?" Matilda asked her younger brother, Archibald. Matilda, at ten, was third in the pecking order.

"Go fish," the seven-year-old Archibald told his redheaded sister. Then he wriggled his nose and wiggled his ears at Emmet, and said, "Your turn."

"I know it's my turn," Emmet answered as he reached for a candy corn. He quickly pulled his cards to his chest when he spotted Archibald trying to peek at his hand. Card playing was not Emmet's idea of fun. If not for the afternoon thunderstorm, he would have been in the woods exploring, or hanging out in his tree fort with his pet monkey, Senator. "How about you, Holly?" Emmet turned to the matriarch of the group. "Got any queens?"

"Rats," Holly said. "I just drew one." She puffed her roly-poly cheeks and plucked the card from her hand. She was twelve. She disliked losing. It went against her cowgirl code.

"Archibald, got any jacks?" Emmet continued.

"Go fish." Archibald went cross-eyed. For a moment it appeared as if he was going to disrupt the card game with a performance of his famous chicken dance—but then he sat back in his chair.

"Are you sure?" Emmet looked sternly at Archibald.

"Sure I'm sure." Archibald projected his lower lip.

As Emmet reached to draw, Matilda sighed and laid her cards down on the table. "I wonder what sort of surprise Great-Aunt Emma Bean is bringing us."

"Matilda is musing again." Holly's curly dark locks jiggled as she laughed at her own joke. Actually, it was not much of a joke; Matilda had an abundant imagination, with which she often mused. She and Holly were opposites. Holly was a doer, not a thinker.

Matilda ignored Holly. "Well, whatever her surprise, I'm sure it will be most magnificent."

"We're not even sure she's coming," Emmet remarked, plucking another candy corn from the bowl.

"She is too, Emmet! You saw the postcard," Matilda reminded him. "It said: 'Expect me at sunset on the first of June. I'm bringing a surprise.' The first is tomorrow."

"I wonder how she's coming?" said Holly.

Archibald suddenly broke into song: "She'll be riding six white horses when she comes, oh yeah. She'll be riding six white horses when she comes. Ooohhh . . . she'll be—"

"Will you grow up?" Holly scoffed.

"That'd be a miracle," Emmet said.

"I'll say," Matilda agreed.

"Bullfrogs!" Archibald pushed his chair back and threw his cards on the table. "Why don't you three grow down?" he huffed, before stomping out of the kitchen and joining his parents on the porch.

"Whatcha doing, Arch?" Henry asked.

"Nothing now. We *were* playing Fish, but they aggravationed me, so I quit."

"You mean aggravated, don't you, Archibald?" said Clementine.

"That's right." Archibald sidled over to the swing and squeezed between his parents. They moved apart to accommodate him. "Mom," he said.

"Yes, Archibald?"

"Do you really think Great-Aunt Emma is coming tomorrow?"

"I do."

"I hope she likes me." Archibald yawned.

"I'm sure she will." Clementine put her arm around her son.

"Good," he said as he sleepily closed his eyes.

The next morning Matilda was up early. She climbed into her bibbed overalls, then stepped lightly from the bedroom she shared with Holly. On her way out, she passed through the kitchen and picked up the bag of snacks she had prepared the night before. The grass was wet with dew as she and Goosebumps left the yard and headed toward the pine woods.

Goosebumps was her confidant. They had been inseparable since the day she'd found him abandoned as a puppy. He had one blue eye and one green one. She named him Goosebumps because that was what she'd gotten when she first saw him.

Matilda was feeling anxious about Great-Aunt Emma Bean's pending arrival. It was her hope that time would pass more quickly in the woods than back at the house. As they walked through the front field, she shared her thoughts with Goosebumps. He plodded dutifully along behind her with an ear lifted to catch every word. "Mom said Great-Aunt Emma Bean is a redhead like me. I can't wait to meet her. Just imagine, Goosebumps—she's a real vagabond. And you know, I don't care what surprise she brings. I just want to shake her hand."

Matilda was not the only Dither who spent an anxious day. Henry had long been mystified by Clementine's foreign aunt. He was just a tad jealous of his wife's fascination with her. There were many mornings on which she spoke of having seen Emma in a dream. It always reminded him of the summer when Clementine had left him and gone to Iceland. He was concerned that somehow the old woman had known how weirdly he'd behaved, and that she now harbored a prejudiced opinion of him. Also, Henry had been wondering how he could possibly express his gratitude for Emma's having given them the farm. He tried to relax by reminding himself that Emma was now his cousin.

Clementine was also a little anxious. Fourteen years had passed since her trip. In that time she and Emma had exchanged occasional letters, but even so, Clementine did not feel in close touch. She was unsure of what to expect. The postcard announcing Emma's arrival had come as a surprise the month before. It had said nothing about her plans. Clementine added the years since they had seen each other, and wondered to what degree her aunt might have aged. It was a long way from Iceland. She hoped Emma would not arrive exhausted by the journey.

Holly spent most of the day practicing show stunts on her all-white pony, Dan. She wanted to be sharp when she had the opportunity to display her equestrian skills for her aunt Emma. It was Holly's dream to one day become a famous rodeo rider.

Emmet did not give Aunt Emma much thought. He and Senator spent the day rooting through an old dump they had recently located. They were searching for artifacts to install in Senator's tree-fort home. They had been collecting together ever since Leopold Hillacre had purchased Senator, a rhesus monkey, from a janitor who worked in a medical lab, and given him to Emmet as a gift. Leopold had already named the monkey. As he explained to the grateful Emmet, "He's smarter than most politicians."

Archibald, like Emmet, got into the rhythm of his day and forgot about Great-Aunt Emma Bean. In the morning he captured crayfish from the creek and put them in a jar with a salamander and a newt. After lunch he hiked to Aylor's Store and shot a round of marbles with his buddy Carl Plummers.

After supper, as the clan gathered expectantly on the front porch, everyone's anxiety level rose a couple of notches. It was visually evident that they were prepared for an important guest. Holly wore her homemade Annie Oakley outfit. She had a touch of liner above her eyelashes, and the blush in her chubby cheeks was enhanced with rouge. Emmet had scrubbed in the tub. His hands were clean and his hair was slicked sideways with cream. At Emmet's behest, Senator wore a bowler hat. Matilda had changed from her overalls into red slacks and a yellow blouse. Even Archibald had spiffed up. He wore black shoes, blue shorts, and a white button-down shirt. Henry looked the same as Archibald, except that he had on trousers instead of shorts. Clementine wore her favorite cotton dress, upon which was pinned a sprig of late-blooming lilac.

As a unit the Dithers were unusually quiet. It was possible that one of them sensed Emma Bean's arrival would initiate a few changes; perhaps one or two suspected a disruption in routine; but it was unlikely that any guessed just how different their lives would soon become. How were they to know they were poised on the brink of a summer during which the normal, tranquil order of their lives would be disrupted by a series of fantastic events? No one warned them that they were sitting in the calm before a storm called Hurricane Emma.

Henry trained a pair of binoculars on a distant point where the driveway disappeared around a bend. "She should be here soon," he said. As the minutes passed and night began to win its battle with day, the idea that Emma might not appear made its rounds on the porch. "She hasn't been here in years," Henry worried aloud. "There's no moon in the sky tonight—I hope she can find the place okay in the dark. Emma did say the first, didn't she?" he asked no one in particular. The Dithers waited in silence for several more minutes. "She would choose the night of the new moon," Henry muttered as he squinted through the binoculars. Suddenly he leaned forward. Everyone on the porch waited as he adjusted the lenses. After a suspenseful moment he announced: "I've got something. Yep. Yep. It's her all right."

"Great-Aunt Emma?"

"I believe so. And . . . it's difficult to be certain in this light, but it looks as though she has a midget with her."

"A midget!" Archibald squealed. "How tall?"

"No. Hold on a second," Henry corrected himself. "Sorry. It's just a boy. Aunt Emma has a boy with her."

"A boy!" Holly cried. "How old?"

"I don't know. Ten, twelve . . . somewhere in there."

"Now that is interesting," Holly observed.

"Let me see," said Clementine.

Henry handed the binoculars to Clementine. He was about to tell his children to run and greet the guests, but only his wife was there to listen. The kids had already departed.

The Dither delegation stood on the inside of the gate and watched Aunt Emma and her companion approach in the twilight. Emma held a suitcase in one hand, and under her arm she carried what looked like a rolled-up rug. The boy had a duffel bag slung over his shoulder. They stopped at the gate. Emma was the first to speak. "I can see I'm at the right place. Clementine did a fine job describing each of you in her letters."

"Hi."

"You must be Holly." Emma pointed.

"Yes, I am," Holly said.

"And you're Matilda." Emma pointed again.

"Welcome to Dither Farm, Aunt Emma." Matilda stepped forward and stretched her hand over the gate. It was grasped and shaken.

"Emmet, right?" Emma met his eye. "You're a little taller than I imagined."

"I've been growing." Emmet nodded.

"Which means you have to be Archibald."

"Yep. I'm me." Archibald grinned back.

"Well, you look like a fine group." Emma Bean beamed with pleasure and rested her hand on the head of the boy at her side. Square shouldered and stout, with a strong jaw and brown, wavy hair, he rubbed sleep from his brown eyes and glanced shyly over the gate. "This is Warren Robinson," Emma said.

"Hi, Warren."

"Howdy."

"Warren might be staying here for a while," Emma continued. "If it suits your folks, of course."

"It's probably okay."

"How old are you?" Holly asked the visitor.

"Almost twelve," Warren answered. And then, bursting with curiosity: "Is that a monkey over there with a hat on?"

"Yeah. He's mine," Emmet boasted.

"Neat. What's his name?"

"Senator. You can touch him if you want."

"Excellent." Warren came fully awake.

"May we help carry your luggage?" Matilda asked as she opened the gate. "Mom and Dad are waiting for you at the house."

"Very kind of you, Matilda," replied Aunt Emma. "Here, you may carry my carpet. Be careful, my dear; it's very special."

Clementine and Henry waited in the side yard. An overhead spotlight illuminated the area. As soon as the party stepped into the circle of light, Clementine rushed forward. "Aunt Emma!"

"Clementine!" They embraced. Emma sniffed the lilac pinned to Clementine's dress. "Oooh. So sweet. Wonderful to see you, dear."

"Thanks. I'm thrilled you're here." Clementine stepped back and turned. "Emma, this is Henry Dither. My husband."

"Pleased to meet you, Henry." Emma extended her right hand.

"The pleasure is mine, Miss Bean." Henry shook the proffered hand and nodded respectfully.

"Good going." Emma winked at Clementine. "Not only is he handsome, but he seems to be a gentleman, too. Speaking of which—come here, Warren—I want you to meet Mr. and Mrs. Dither. Warren is the son of some recently deceased friends of mine from New Hampshire."

Warren stepped forward.

"Nice to meet you, Warren," Clementine said.

"It's my pleasure to meet you, ma'am," Warren replied. After a small, dignified bow, he turned to Henry and spoke in the most grown-up voice he could muster. "Hello, Mr. Dither. I'm a farmer too. So don't hesitate to ask if you need any help around here."

"Very good of you to offer," Henry replied in a respectful tone. "I'll certainly keep that in mind."

Later, after refreshments and snacks, the Dithers held their two visitors hostage in the living room, where everyone took turns asking and answering questions. Great-Aunt Emma did most of the answering, and contrary to Clementine's concern that her aunt would arrive at the farm in an exhausted state, the old lady was full of pep. She seemed genuinely delighted to be with the family, and responded cheerfully to the barrage of inquiries fired at her from around the room. Somehow, as she fielded the numerous and varied questions, she made everyone feel she was speaking directly to him or her. Henry was charmed. He sat opposite her, spellbound by her rich voice, observing every gesture she made. All of his previous concerns had vanished. He could see by the way she related to the children that she was a good person. Probably can't help it if she is mysterious, he thought. Which is exactly what Clementine was thinking—mysterious. As far as she could tell, Emma Bean had not aged a day since Clementine had last seen her in the airport in Reykjavík. If anything, she seemed younger than before.

The welcoming party broke up at midnight. Warren was put in the second bed in Emmet's room, and Archibald was moved downstairs to a cot in the pantry. The arrangement agreed with Warren and Emmet. Long before they drifted off to sleep that night, they made a pact to be best pals. Emmet had never had a best pal his own age. He was so moved with the idea, he took Warren into his confidence and offered to lead him to a secret pool he knew about, located deep in the heart of Weeping Willow Swamp. Emmet had been there only once, during a drought, with Leopold Hillacre. Nevertheless, he felt confident he could find the spot again. "I'm telling ya, Warren," Emmet whispered in the darkness. "The bullfrogs in that pool are as big as your head."

"Amazing." Warren yawned. "I've never seen one bigger than a softball."

42

As Holly and Matilda prepared for bed, they discussed the visitor from New Hampshire.

"He's a dream," Holly said. "He was sent here by angels."

"He is very polite," Matilda noted. "Did you hear him offer to help Dad on the farm?"

"I heard every word he uttered." Holly sighed longingly.

"He seems shy."

"That wasn't shyness. It was maturity."

"Do you think his hair is naturally wavy like that, or do you think he had it done?"

"I'm sure it's natural," Holly said with conviction as she fell back on her bed. She flopped her arms out and exclaimed, "Can you believe he's sleeping right under our own roof!"

After everyone else was in bed, Clementine and Emma sat in the kitchen and chatted. After an exchange of compliments about how well the other looked, Clementine asked about Warren. "Did you say his parents were deceased?"

"Yes, I did," Emma said sadly. "It's been almost a year now since they died. It was an automobile accident."

"I'm so sorry to hear that," Clementine said sincerely.

"I'll miss them. They were some of the finest people I ever knew. Warren is so much like his father."

"Poor boy." Clementine didn't know what to say.

"I was his godmother, and have custody of him now. He has no other family, so I stayed with him in New Hampshire while the estate was settled. He really is a good egg, Clementine. He's adjusting pretty well . . . but I'll have to be returning to Iceland soon, and I'm not sure that'll be the best place for him to grow up."

"Hmmm," Clementine hemmed thoughtfully. "So, Emma, what's on your agenda? I do hope you'll be staying for a while."

"Unfortunately, dear, I have to leave the day after tomorrow for

Washington. I've been hired by the State Department to teach a course. It runs for five weeks."

"What sort of course?"

"A training program I developed. It's called Sharp."

"Which means . . . ?"

"Sharp is an acronym. It stands for Subliminal Hypnogenetic And Retentivity Principles. It was designed for intelligence agents and diplomats. The curriculum deals with enhancing a person's ability to gather information in the field. Sorry, that's all I can tell you. Confidential, you understand."

Clementine nodded silently. She did not understand.

"So I'll be stuck in Washington for over a month," Emma said regretfully, "which leaves me concerned about Warren. I was wondering, Clementine, if it was at all possible—"

Clementine was quick to offer. "Emma, please, we'd be happy to keep Warren for as long as you like. Not to worry."

"Thank you." Emma patted Clementine on the arm and smiled warmly. "I knew I could count on you."

"Honestly, Emma, I'm glad to help."

Emma shifted in her seat. "There is one more small favor . . ."

"Whatever—just ask."

"I need a safe place to leave my carpet. It's a rare and valuable antique. Museum quality. I suppose I could cart it with me to D.C. if there's no good place here."

"No problem. I know just the spot. We'll put it under the bed in the room where Henry and I sleep. No one will bother it there. The kids aren't allowed in our room."

"Under the bed?" Emma was doubtful.

"Safe as any bank," Clementine said confidently. "Henry and I have been keeping our nest egg there since we were first married. I'm sure your carpet will be fine."

five

IN KEEPING WITH HER habit, Matilda rose early in the morning, put on her overalls, made her bed, and tiptoed down the stairs. She had peaches and cornflakes on her mind. It surprised her to see her mother and great-aunt Emma sitting at the kitchen table. Matilda knew in a glance that they had been up all night. Her first thought was one of envy: How interesting it would have been to hear what passed between them! Her next thought was one of approval: Her own mother participated in an all-nighter with a world-traveling gypsy queen! (That is how Matilda had begun to think of her great-aunt.) She was welcomed with a pair of good-morning kisses.

Before she had time to sit down and join the two older women in a moment of privacy, there was a stirring in the pantry and Archibald was awake. He made a squeaky noise, then shuffled into the kitchen wearing underpants only. He yawned, scratched his belly, and looked up at the ceiling as a series of thumps and thuds reverberated off the floor above. It was Henry getting out of bed and putting on his work boots. He had coffee on his mind as he clomped downstairs. Next the door on the second floor creaked open as Emmet and Warren entered the hall. Soon everyone was gathered in the kitchen except Holly. She remained in bed hugging a pillow. She was dreaming about a cowboy from New Hampshire.

Clementine announced to all present in the kitchen that there would be a cookout in the evening to honor Great-Aunt Emma Bean's visit. She informed Emmet that he and Warren would have to postpone their bullfrog expedition, and sent him instead to Aylor's Store with a grocery list and an invitation for Jimmy and Alice to come to the farm around suppertime. Archibald was dispatched to Leopold Hillacre's with a similar invitation, as well as instructions for Leopold to pass the word to Flea Jenfries. Matilda and Emma planned to spend the morning visiting Clementine's parents at Gooden Farm. Henry, as usual, went to work in his fields. Clementine, a bit weary, went up to her bedroom to get a few hours of sleep. Before she turned in, she stuck her head into Holly's room and asked her if she would be good enough to show Warren around the farm.

"You want me to make him feel welcome?" Holly sat up in bed with her eyes wide open. "Oh, I'll make him comfortable if I have to chain him to a rock to do it."

As it occurred, she did not have to chain Warren to a rock, but she did render him immobile with a program of daring stunts. He sat riveted to a log as Dan, traveling at breakneck speed, galloped around him in circles while Holly switched from standing frontward, to swinging sideways, to hanging under Dan's belly, to sitting backward. She ended her performance by spinning from a hand-lift dismount into a double cartwheel.

"Way to go!" Warren applauded. "I've never seen anyone ride like that. Especially not a girl. You should go on television."

Clementine slept much longer than she had intended. When she awoke, it was early in the afternoon. As she sat up, she was aware of a strange dream slipping from her conscious mind. In the dream Henry had been zooming down a hill in a small, open vehicle when suddenly a large man leaped from nowhere and knocked him from it. She recalled seeing her husband tumble across the ground, and curiously she had felt relieved. An odd dream. It made no sense. Perhaps, thought Clementine, sleeping in the day causes strange dreams. Normally at this time her mind was busy with an array of concerns—about the children, her pregnancy, the farm, the cider business, the weather. Now, as she climbed out of bed, she found herself thinking of Emma Bean and the time she had spent in Iceland. She knew she had enjoyed the visit, and she knew she had grown during her stay, but all she could recall actually doing there was sitting with her aunt on the porch. Why could she not remember the details of her trip?

Blood rushed to Clementine's head as she bent to look under the bed for her shoes. When the tingling in her face subsided, her mind shifted from the dreamy past back to the present moment. She wondered if Emmet was back with the groceries, and she began creating a menu for the cookout. She noted that Leopold Hillacre was fond of salad, and that Jimmy Aylor was virtually addicted to her sweet-potato pie. She thought about napkins and paper plates, and which utensils she would need. As she started down the stairs, she was thinking about where to put the chairs in the yard. It was back to business as usual. She was Mom again.

Flea Jenfries was the first guest to arrive. Henry was in the yard preparing the charcoal grill when she drove up in her dependable old station wagon. She wore a green jumpsuit with a matching green headband. She looked a bit like a grasshopper.

"Hello, handsome," Flea hailed Henry as she approached.

"Hi, Flea. Gain some weight?" he asked. It was a running joke between them.

"I'm up to ninety-six now," she replied.

"Gracious! Keep on like that and you'll soon catch up with Bellamonte Smoot."

"Don't make me laugh," Flea snorted. "Now, where are your wife and that Bean woman I've been wanting to meet?"

"In the kitchen." Henry pointed with a spatula.

After Flea was inside, Henry heard Alice and Jimmy Aylor approaching in Jimmy's modified '49 Ford. Emmet, Warren, and Senator rushed into the yard to admire the powerful machine. It rumbled to a halt beside Flea's station wagon, then backfired as Jimmy switched off the ignition. Senator screeched and bolted up the nearest tree.

"Sorry I scared your monkey," Jimmy said to Emmet as he stepped out of the car. Jimmy had on his trademark plaid pants.

"He gets spooked by loud noises," Emmet explained.

Jimmy walked around and opened the door for his portly wife, Alice. She was laughing as she stepped from the car. "I thought that primate was gonna jump right out of his skin."

Leopold Hillacre arrived late. The children had already been served. Holly, who sat perched on top of a fence post while she ate, spotted the old bachelor in the distance. He moved in the general direction of the house, but zigzagged wildly in his approach. He darted twenty yards to the left, twenty to the right, doubled back ten, then ten ahead.

"Here comes Leopold," Holly heralded. "Either there's a bee after him, or he's chasing a butterfly."

Sure enough, when Leopold finally appeared at the fence he was red in the face and was carrying a butterfly net.

"Sorry I'm tardy." He waved to everyone at once. "I got distracted by a Baltimore checkerspot. A real beauty. I'd been following her since the bridge."

"Come eat," Henry called.

"But first come here," Clementine said. "I have someone I would like you to meet."

"Yup." Leopold leaped over the fence with an agility belying his seventy-three years. He was a tall, slender man with a towering forehead and a long, broad nose. Heavy lines crisscrossed his weathered face, bespeaking years spent out-of-doors. At a glance he gave the impression of being a tough old goat, yet on closer inspection the harshness was mitigated by the profusion of wispy white hair hovering tenuously above his head. The gathering of white contrasted sharply with his bright, bluer-than-blue eyes. His image was additionally cushioned by his soft-spoken, mild manners. Many women found him attractive in a hand-hewn, original sort of way.

Clementine laid a hand on her aunt's shoulder. "Aunt Emma, meet Leopold Whaddamidge Hillacre. His ancestors settled in Willow County in the seventeenth century." Clementine turned. "Leopold, my cousin from Iceland: Miss Emma Alderson Bean."

"A genuine pleasure, miss." Leopold clicked his heels.

"Baltimore checkerspot. Is that what you call a *Melitaea phaëton?*" Emma smiled and extended her small hand.

"Yes. It is indeed." Leopold clasped her fingers and shook delicately. "I'll be . . . you are a lepidopterist?"

"Merely an amateur, I assure you."

"But a well-informed amateur, and a pretty one at that."

"You're being kind."

"Just honest . . . Miss Bean." The old bachelor bowed his head in an effort to hide his own blushing.

Flea slapped her knee and giggled gayly. "I do believe Leopold is flirting."

Alice chuckled along. "There's sugar in his voice."

"You two hush." Jimmy looked askance at Flea and his wife.

"Let me fix you some salad," said Clementine, rising and grabbing Leopold by the elbow.

"Yes. Thank you, Clementine. Salad would suit me fine." He

49

allowed himself to be directed toward the serving table, but he kept the eyes in the back of his head focused on the attractive guest from Iceland. He was thrilled to sense that she was watching as he filled his plate.

Clementine's dinner party proceeded smoothly. There were no overturned dishes nor bees in the butter pats. The children were relatively civilized during the meal and did not disturb the adults until afterward, when they began to clamor for dessert. Yet they were not reprimanded for their noisy insistence. Clementine's sweet-potato pie topped with homemade whipped cream and wild strawberries had the adults clamoring too. Even Senator climbed out of his tree and indulged in a slice.

After the dessert plates were licked and put away, the children congregated on the front porch and played Fish, while Henry, Jimmy, and (reluctantly) Leopold went behind the barn and tossed horseshoes. Alice, Flea, Clementine, and Emma were left alone to talk. The Willowite women quite naturally deferred to the older, well-traveled Emma Bean. They were curious about anything she would tell them. She had lived in and seen the wide world, while they (except for Clementine's one trip) had hardly left Willow County. Emma was attuned to her audience; she did her best to encapsulate. "Mostly," she began, "the world is just a little town repeated over and over. Languages vary, and in cities the towns are densely clustered in blocks, but overall it is the same everywhere. There are good people, bad people, and boring people." Emma put an emphasis on "boring" and made a dreary expression as she spoke. The women all laughed. Flea especially so.

"Well, bless any town with a Crystal Hooper," she said. "You talk boring—Crystal can kill ya with lack of interest."

Leopold could hear the women laughing. The sound filled him with envy. He wanted to shuck his horseshoe and join the gals, but an ingrained sense of male propriety held him back.

"Of course," Emma continued, "ironies do exist. Or worse than ironies: apathetic crimes. There are places where children starve to death every day. Real children, with real mothers." Emma's face formed an angry mask. "Yet meanwhile, there are other places where weight-loss clinics are a booming business."

The idea of even one baby, anywhere, going hungry—much less starving—angered the women from Willow. Had they not been so satiated with supper and so content with their own good company, they might have organized a political action committee and fomented a revolution. As it was, they sat with long faces and felt ashamed to be human. Emma saw what she had done, and in order to change the mood she humored the women with a story about a handsome philanthropist she had recently met. "Yes, very," she replied to one question. "Yes, a bachelor," she replied to the next. "Oh, no indeed," she replied to the last.

Later, as the evening was drawing to a close and the guests were bidding their adieus, Leopold Hillacre approached Emma Bean and asked her straight out: "Do you cast spells?"

"Mr. Hillacre." Emma feigned shock.

"I have to tell you, Miss Bean, I've been smitten by something this evening, and my feeling is that you have much to do with it."

"I don't know what you mean," Emma said.

Leopold cleared his throat. "If I may be so bold. I have never met anyone like you. I hope when you return from Washington you'll find time to visit my home and see my collections."

"I do adore butterflies." Emma smiled openly. "I shall look forward to visiting."

"I also have a collection of oriental carpets, antique books, and fossils I found myself," Leopold added, beaming.

"You do!" Emma warmed her voice a notch. "I am extremely fascinated by carpets."

Leopold wriggled his nose and muttered, "Yes, well. I am fascinated by you."

*   *   *

The following morning Clementine, Henry, and Emma Bean climbed into the blue cab of Henry's 1951 Chevrolet pickup and drove to Binkerton. Henry loved his truck. He fed it Marvel Mystery Oil and changed the filters three times a year. He talked to it going up hills. It was one of those postwar, let's-make-'em-to-last farm trucks capable of talking back.

Emma parted company with the Dithers at the bus depot in downtown Binkerton. She rode the bus from there to the Amtrack station in Bricksburg, where she boarded *The Colonial* heading north to Union Station in Washington, D.C. She took the Metro from Union Station to Dupont Circle and then hailed a taxi to the Mayflower Hotel on Connecticut Avenue. She loitered in the lobby until three fifty-two in the afternoon, when a short man wearing a toupee, carrying a folded *Wall Street Journal* under his left arm, and sporting a carnation in his lapel approached her for a match. When she produced a Zippo instead of a match, the man glanced furtively around the lobby and whispered: "The name is Reynolds. Follow me." She did. A limousine was waiting for them outside. It whisked them to an address in Foggy Bottom, slowed for a visual check at a security gate, then disappeared into the bowels of an underground garage.

six

THE DAY AFTER EMMA'S departure, Emmet, Warren, and Senator went on their expedition into Weeping Willow Swamp. When they left the farm early in the morning, an ominous blanket of nimbostratus clouds darkened the horizon. They considered postponing their trip, but not seriously. They chose instead to take their chances and turn around later if necessary. The clouds soon thinned, and they forgot about the threat of rain. They marched single file, with Emmet in the lead and Senator in the rear. Emmet carried a machete in a sheath. It was attached to his hip with twine. Slung over his shoulders was a knapsack containing the essentials: rope, matches, firecrackers, gum, sandwiches, fruit, and a thermos filled with Tang. The fruit was for Senator. As Emmet explained to Warren: "It pays to keep your monkey happy when traveling through a swamp."

They hiked three miles through the woods until they reached Leopold Hillacre's property, where they turned north and hiked another mile before entering the forest on the east side of the swamp. Emmet halted the expedition while they were still on solid ground. He looked Warren over as if to size him up, then cleared his throat and solemnly advised, "Better stick with me in there. It can get tricky. You might have a few marshes in New Hampshire, but they wouldn't amount to a mud puddle next to this baby."

"Right. I'll stay close."

"Senator will be our advance scout. He'll let us know if we're heading into a briar patch or about to wade into quicksand."

"Quicksand?" Warren peered ahead.

"It's in there. But you have to be pretty stupid to get caught in it." Emmet scoffed at the thought.

"Still, it's nice to have a scout."

"Senator's the best. Aren't you, buddy?" Emmet smiled at his monkey. Senator crossed his arms and smiled back. Then Emmet announced, "We should cut our jammers now."

"Jammers?"

"You know. Snake sticks. Get a strong one with a crook at the end. Makes it easier to deal with 'em."

"Deal with . . . snakes?"

"Only if necessary. It's best just to leave them alone. But a jammer is good for lots of things. You can walk with it raised out in front of you and it'll snatch spiderwebs from between the branches before they get on your face."

Warren nodded. "Old Indian trick. I've used it before. I just didn't know you called them jammers."

"One last note," Emmet said seriously. "If you see any wild pigs, don't hesitate. Get up the first tree you think will hold you. Hopefully a comfortable one. And don't come down until I say it's safe. Got that?"

"Got it."

"Good. Now don't worry about a thing." Emmet slapped his new pal on the shoulder. "Some people get spooked in a swamp, but then some people are afraid of their own shadows. We might get wet, but it'll be worth it."

"Bullfrogs, here we come!"

At the same time the adventurers were sallying forth into the foreboding expanse of Weeping Willow Swamp, their expedition was being discussed back on Dither Farm. Or rather, Holly was discussing Warren. "I wonder where they are right now," she said to Matilda. "It looks like it might rain. They'll get soaked if it rains. I don't know why Emmet insisted on taking Warren into that swamp on his third day here. Dumb boy stuff, if you ask me. Do you think it will rain, Matilda? You're usually good at guessing that."

"I don't know," Matilda answered without lifting her eyes from the book she was reading on oriental carpets. After carrying Aunt Emma's rug, she had become interested in carpets and gone to the library in Binkerton, where she'd withdrawn several titles on the subject.

"I'm pretty sure Warren has a crush on me," Holly continued. "Yesterday he said I ought to be a movie star."

"Hmmm."

"He recommended I go on television first. He thought for sure I'd be a hit."

"Anything's possible," Matilda murmured.

"It usually takes an outsider to notice."

"Notice what?" Matilda looked up.

"Star quality. Either you have it or you don't," Holly explained. "Warren is sensitive enough to see it in a girl."

A minute later, when Archibald entered the room, Matilda was buried deeper in her book and Holly was hugging a pillow and staring into space. "She eat a horse tranquilizer?" he asked.

"Naw," Matilda said. "She's just in another one of her Dale Evans moods. Only Roy Rogers is off with Emmet."

"Oh. Oh yeah, Matilda. May I take Goosebumps with me to

Aylor's Store? I'm going to shoot marbles with Carl."

"Fine, Archibald. Just make sure he doesn't get his head in behind the meat counter again. Dad said I'd have to pay for it if Goosebumps ate any more steaks."

Weeping Willow Swamp covers approximately five square miles of Willow County. That might not sound like much, until you consider that it equals three thousand, two hundred acres of mucky, spongy, uncertain, overgrown terrain. If acreage seems vague, imagine you were lost in there with no sense of direction, at night (God forbid); then you might come to think of the place as one hundred thirty-nine million, three hundred and ninety-two thousand square feet of treacherous, slimy bog.

Two major streams pass north to south through the swamp and empty into the wide floodplain of the Mattaponi River. To the west is Polecat Creek, the deeper and larger of the two streams. It is infested with leeches and snapping turtles. Approximately a half mile east of Polecat Creek, flowing more or less in a straight line through the center of the swamp, is Bustle Branch. It is swift and shallow. At the south end of the swamp, where the two streams merge, there is a scrub forest so dense with briars that rabbits must follow paths to pass through. Supposedly there are several ponds in this forest where geese and ducks abound, but only Leopold Hillacre traveling in his hot-air balloon has ever seen them. The western edge of the swamp is met by a wall of hills that roll eastward from a high plateau until they pitch radically and crumble into black thickets along the slippery banks of Polecat Creek. Leopold's place is at the south end of these western hills, near a small road running between the swamp and the river. In the north lie the springs that are the headwaters of Bustle Branch. Access is restricted by steep, thickly vegetated ravines. It is near these springs, which gurgle up amid clusters of weeping-willow trees, that the bullfrog pools exist. Emmet considered entering from the north, but it meant continuing the hike an extra four miles just to reach the ravines. Instead he decided to enter the swamp from the east, where the forest was flat and relatively void of troublesome undergrowth. Although there was more swamp to cross, it seemed like the most expedient route.

By ten fifteen, after a detour to peruse an old dump, the trio had reached the edge of the forest and were standing upon a moss-covered spit of land that jutted into a smelly quagmire of black muck.

"Looks like the world died right here," Warren said.

"It's not a very pretty sight," Emmet agreed. "From here on in, it's gonna be interesting. Senator." He snapped his fingers. It was a signal for Senator to take the lead. As the little fellow scampered past Warren on his way to the front, he looked up with the proud expression of an officer assigned to an important reconnaissance mission. Senator knew the swamp was serious business. He accepted it as a credit to his genus that he, a *Macaca mulatta*, would now be making critical decisions for two *Homo sapiens*.

From this point onward the trio measured their progress in short, sometimes daring clump-to-clump, island-to-island, foot-to-handhold leaps. With Senator ranging twenty to fifty yards ahead, stopping occasionally to gesticulate directions, they progressed one half of a mile in an hour. During that time they swung on vines over mud flats, pole-vaulted across ditches, and crossed fallen-log bridges over deep ravines. When necessary, they waded in murky water. Assuming they kept a steady pace, Emmet figured they would reach the pool by two P.M., admire the giant amphibians, and be back at Dither Farm in time for supper at seven.

What he did not figure on was rain.

Henry had driven to his old friend Garland Barlow's to borrow an augur for his tractor and was standing outside Garland's toolshed when he heard a rumble in the distance. Garland was inside the shed, sorting through his tools. "Was that thunder?" Henry asked.

"What?" said Garland. "I can't hear much in here."

Henry spoke louder. "It was thunder all right."

"You wonder if you might what?" asked Garland.

"Never mind," Henry hollered, then, "The timing is just right for my beans."

"What?" Garland said. "You're getting ripe for greens?"

"Nothing, Garland!" Henry shouted.

"Found it," Garland called. Henry could hear tools falling and clanging together. At the same time there was another rumble of distant thunder in the west. Garland stepped out of the shed with the augur in his hands and glanced up at the darkening sky. "It sure enough looks like rain," he observed.

Emmet, Warren, and Senator were near Bustle Branch, a half mile from where Emmet estimated the pools to be, when an angry boom echoed in the sky and a lightning bolt crackled down to earth. Thirty feet from where the boys were standing a stump suddenly exploded. Senator scampered off into the dense brush.

"Damn!" Emmet cursed. "We better start back." He cupped his hands and called, "SENATOR!" Before the sound of his voice had faded, raindrops began to fall. "Let's find cover."

Emmet and Warren backtracked a hundred yards to where a solitary walnut tree stood on a patch of high ground. As they ran under its boughs, a second bolt of lightning flashed over the swamp and the storm formally commenced. Within a matter of seconds so much water was falling that visibility was limited to fifty feet. Emmet knew it was unwise to stay under a tall tree when lightning was striking, but it was either that or stand in the open and be pelted by driving rain and hail.

The rain drilled Willow County for over an hour without a hint of surcease. Emmet and Warren were only partially protected. A drizzle penetrated the overhead foliage and descended upon them without mercy. Wisely, Emmet had kept the knapsack dry. He withdrew from it two peanut-butter-and-jelly sandwiches. He handed one to Warren. Both boys were tired, muddy, scratched, and wet . . . yet neither complained as they wolfed down the sandwiches. After washing down the peanut butter with Tang, they stared silently into the downpour and kept company with their own thoughts.

Henry was feeling good about life as he parked his truck in the barn and unloaded the borrowed augur. The rain was right on schedule. He had little to do now except sit back and enjoy the excellent wibberniffling weather. He kicked up his heels and sang, "Oh, give me the farmer's life! It's as good as the farmer's wife! There's never a day of strife! Oh, give me the farmer's life!"

Clementine was standing at the sink, staring out the window, when Henry bounded into the kitchen. He could see in a glance that she was troubled. "Why the long face?" he asked.

"Emmet and Warren went into Weeping Willow Swamp this morning. I'm afraid they're going to have an awful time getting out in this mess."

"I'd forgotten they were going. But don't worry. Emmet has plenty of horse sense. I bet they're over at Leopold's place."

"I wish that man would get a telephone! The boys could be lost. You can't see ten feet ahead out there."

"Did they take Senator?"

"Yes."

"Then I doubt they're lost."

"Henry, I don't have as much faith in that monkey as you do. People have been lost in that swamp during droughts."

"Where's Archibald?"

"At the store. Jimmy called a while ago to say he'd bring him home when the rain lets up."

"I'll swing by and get him. Now please, don't worry about the boys." Henry stepped forward and hugged his wife.

59

Except for the sound of rain hitting leaves, the boys had been sitting for two silent hours when Warren, who was standing to stretch his legs, jumped backward and shouted, "HEY, EMMET! Is that a snake in the tree?"

"Where?" Emmet jumped to his feet.

"Right there." Warren pointed to a low-hanging branch.

"Oh, no," Emmet moaned. "It's a moccasin. A very bad sign."

"Bad luck?"

"Worse than that. Moccasins climb trees only when there's going to be a flood."

"Damn." Warren showed he too could curse.

"Hell damn." Emmet doubled the curse. "I wonder where Senator is. We can't wait for him any longer. We gotta go. Now."

"I'm right behind you."

Emmet and Warren, running for all they were worth, attempted to retrace their path back toward the eastern forest. Rain pounded at their backs as they slipped and slid forward. After they had gone about a thousand yards, Warren looked up and remarked, "I don't remember a lake."

"It wasn't there before. We'll have to go around it. That way, away from the river." Emmet did not delay. "Come on."

After twenty more minutes the downpour had diminished from a deluge to a regular rainfall, making it easier for Emmet and Warren to see as they picked their way through a morass of vines, reeds, and swamp grass. Their feet had long since been submerged, and in many places water reached to their knees. The boys soon arrived at a bit of high ground, where they stopped to catch their breath. They had been resting for about twenty seconds when they were startled by the snap of a tree branch. Both of them whipped around in time to see Senator swooping into view. Looking more like a wet mop than a monkey, he landed at their feet, then screeched, flipped backward, and leaped up into Emmet's open arms. After a quick, affectionate, wet hug, he dropped to the ground and pointed urgently to the south.

Senator didn't wait for debate. He turned and started running. The boys followed hot on his heels.

When Henry arrived at Aylor's Store, he found a congregation of idlers hard at work. Jimmy had a card game going across the meat counter. At a nickel a bet, he dealt blackjack to half a dozen takers. Over by the rotating magazine stand, Garland Barlow perused the latest in fashion. Goosebumps was sleeping in front of the ice-cream freezer. In the rear of the store, amid the dry goods, Archibald and Carl Plummers teamed together in a marbles match against John Washington and Felton Fibbs. The stakes were a penny a point.

Carl Plummers and Jimmy Aylor had been shipmates in the navy. Soon after the war, Carl paid a visit to Willow County. He liked it so much he wound up never leaving. By the time he and Archibald met and became friends, Carl had become a fixture at the store—a large fixture—weighing in excess of four hundred pounds. For most people of this bulk, the bending and stooping demands of shooting marbles would limit their playing time. But not Carl. With Jimmy's help, he had designed and constructed a low-riding, four-wheel contraption upon which he could readily convey himself around the store. It had a spring-loaded tractor seat welded on top of two metal milk crates, which were mounted on the base of a refrigerator frame. Within the confines of the store, Carl had nearly unlimited mobility. He was the reigning marbles champion. The only person who stood a chance of beating him was his best friend and protégé, Archibald Dither. When the two of them teamed together, victory was the inevitable outcome.

Henry watched as Archibald and Carl scored five successive

points against their slightly inebriated opponents. Then he spoke. "Hate to break up your game, son, but I want you to ride with me over to Leopold Hillacre's."

"Sure, Dad. Just let me get that yellow taw over by the flour barrel."

While Archibald was scrutinizing the lay of the floor and lining up his shot, Garland Barlow stepped around the corner.

"Hey, Garland," Henry said.

"Hey, Henry." Garland reached and clasped Henry's shoulder. "Did I hear you say you're going to see Leopold?"

"Yep."

"I just drove by that way, and I barely made it through in my truck. The water is rising fast; by now the road must be flooded over the little bridge."

Henry's face dropped. A hair on his head turned gray.

"What's the matter?" Garland asked.

"Emmet and a friend went into the swamp this morning before it started raining. I want to see if they're with Leopold."

"You'll have to drive around the long way by Campbell Creek. Unless you have a boat. I suppose then you could cross right below the hill there at the house."

"Wade Butcher's got a boat he'll lend me."

"I'm coming with you," said Garland.

Senator led the boys back to Bustle Branch and followed it south. The stream gurgled and clapped as it surged by them, sometimes spilling onto the already-wet land in waves. Yet Senator picked a firm, clear route through the brush, and the trio made rapid progress. They rushed past the spot where they had rested before the storm without pausing to commemorate. The monkey was relentless. He would not slow the pace until they were safely ensconced upon the elevated peninsula where he was heading.

It was a close call. A sweeping tide sucked at their feet as they dragged themselves onto the high ground. Immediately afterward the creek broke from its confines and cut a swath across the shoulder of the peninsula. Contiguous with land no longer, the island was about half the size of a football field, shaped irregularly like a paramecium. Higher up, on the apex of the island, was a stand of loblolly pine growing from an outcropping of rocks and small boulders. The tired, wet trio headed there for a bit of dry shelter.

Before plopping down in exhaustion, Emmet climbed one of the pines and scanned the distance. He did not like what he saw. The swamp had become a turbid sea. He and his mates were marooned on a shrinking hilltop in an archipelago of shrinking islands.

seven

THE RAIN STOPPED in time for the five-o'clock rush hour in Washington, D.C. Emma Bean sat in the backseat of a standard sedan and admired the greenery of Rock Creek Parkway. She was wearing a dark skirt and white blouse, and no makeup, and her rich auburn hair was mostly hidden in a tight bun at the nape of her neck. She did not wish to attract attention.

The driver followed the parkway until he reached the Potomac River, where he turned left, then right, and pulled up in front of the Watergate Hotel. Emma had been assigned an upper-floor apartment. It was not numbered. The balcony afforded a sweeping view from Georgetown across Arlington, past the memorials, and on to National Airport. She liked living near the water. Water always made her feel comfortable. The rain during the day had lifted her spirits.

She closed the door, dropped her briefcase, kicked off her shoes, and rushed toward the balcony. As she pulled back the curtains and stepped outside, a shaft of bright sunlight poked through the cloud cover and threw a golden ray upon the river. She smiled and reached to undo her bun. At the same moment, more than a hundred miles southeast of the Watergate Hotel, a second shaft of sunlight performed a similar act over a swamp somewhere in the Tidewater region of Virginia.

Henry, Garland, Archibald, and Goosebumps arrived at Wade Butcher's trailer at four thirty. By quarter to five they had the rowboat in the pickup and were on their way to the flooded section of road below the swamp. Time, which had previously been so abundant, had suddenly fallen into short supply. When the men arrived at the creek, they found the bridge submerged at both ends. The stream had tripled in size. It had quadrupled in power. When Wade and Garland set the wooden craft upon the raging surface, only quick thinking and muscle saved it from ripping free. They began to wonder how, and if, they would manage to cross.

Leopold Hillacre had been surveying the flood from the cupola atop his barn when Henry and the others arrived at the bridge. He observed the incident with the boat and from his perspective was able to devise a solution. He hurriedly descended the stairs to the tool room on the ground floor of the barn. Here he grabbed a length of rope and two large pulleys. As he ran to assist his friends, he began in his mind to engineer an overhead tramway.

After a lot of hollering back and forth, many extra efforts, and a pound of ingenuity, the rope was finally strung from a tree on Leopold's side to Henry's truck bumper on the other. Using bare hands to grip and pull, the men, along with Archibald and Goosebumps, were then able to cross the rising water. But the accomplishment was of little consolation to Henry. He had already learned from Leopold that his son was not there.

Word traveled fast. By six thirty in the evening, fifty-five percent of the able-bodied adults within a ten-mile radius of Aylor's Store had volunteered to participate in the search effort. Jimmy and Carl had set up a command post in the store and organized the volunteers: two persons in a team, three teams to a unit, four units. Ten women and fourteen men. They may not shoot dead skunks or wear fancy watches in Willow County, but if someone is in real need, they sure know how to hop over fences and lend a hand. The effort to find Emmet and Warren was an expression of their community spirit. Also, in addition to the fifty-five percent who formally volunteered, there was a contingent of loners, independents, and misfits who scoured the wet thickets alone.

Jimmy wiped the produce prices from the chalkboard and drew a rough map of the swamp, dividing it into numbered quadrants. Carl assigned numbers to each team and explained a system by which they were to report back to the store through their unit leaders, whom he appointed. Carl also arranged to have megaphones borrowed from the cheerleading squad at school. Everyone could see his intense concern as he handed out the cardboard cones and ordered each team to go out and find the boys. It was the sensitive side of Carl that few people knew. Suddenly his size, which had previously been a handicap, became a willful force. As the search teams started their vehicles and began to drive away, they could hear his command, "Bring me good news."

Meanwhile, about a mile from the store, on the other side of the woods, across a creek, beyond a cornfield and a pasture, through a stand of tall pines, at the end of a long driveway, someone else was exerting a willful force . . . someone who felt perhaps more concern even than Carl. Usually she was a reserved, soft-spoken person, but now there was a sharp snap in her voice and a fire in her eyes. "I don't care if it's practical or not!" Clementine informed Flea Jenfries and Bellamonte Smoot, who had been trying to persuade her to wait at home. "I'm going to go to Leopold's house right now, even if I have to walk or take the tractor to get there."

"Clementine, you are assuming too much," Flea began. "I'm sure if you'd just wait here for a little—"

"I am not waiting anywhere." Clementine turned to her daughters, who were standing at the kitchen door. They received her with admiring gazes. They had always known she was a strong person, yet they had never seen her utilize her full strength. They were both alarmed—because of the seriousness of the moment—and proud—of their mother's power.

Flea, who knew more about psychology than the girls, felt empathy. She knew Clementine was fighting a maternal fear that would not go away until the boys were safe at home. "Let's go in my wagon." Flea snatched her hat from the table and sprang from her chair.

"Let's," Clementine echoed. Then she shooed Matilda and Holly from the kitchen. "You girls run upstairs and get some towels and blankets. Hurry now and meet us at the car."

Although it is only three miles by crow's flight from Dither Farm to Leopold Hillacre's house, by road, taking the long route past Campbell's Creek, it is a twelve-mile trip. For half of it the group rode in silence, except for the incessant sound of water splashing against the undercarriage of the big blue station wagon. The world they rode through was drenched. Every field, yard, and pasture hosted either a stream, a puddle, a pool, or a pond. In the road were numerous decaying bits of trash that had been vomited from shallow ditches. In all directions trees were splayed and bent. It was not an encouraging sight for someone searching for missing children. Bellamonte could no longer endure the heavy silence. "I love the way the world looks so clean right after a good storm."

"Wild and wrecked to my eye." Clementine smothered a cry.

"Mom, are you all right?" asked Matilda.

Clementine turned toward the backseat. Through a thin film of tears she caressed her daughters with a trembling smile. "I'm fine. Just thinking too much, that's all."

"Dad once said he thought the mind was a dangerous tool," remarked Holly.

"Your father . . ." Clementine's expression softened into a smile, and she laughed. "Your father *is* dangerous when he thinks too much. Especially if he's worried."

"Yeah, we've noticed," Matilda giggled.

"He sure can be weird," Holly chuckled.

It was a little after seven. About an hour and fifteen minutes remained before sunset. From the summit of the shrinking island where they were stranded, Emmet, Warren, and Senator could hear the occasional blast of an auto horn or the echoing report of a far-off shotgun. Once Emmet heard voices drifting through the swamp and thought he could see people walking on the hills in the west. With the hope of drawing their attention, he got the firecrackers and matches from the knapsack and attempted to sound a blast. But moisture had seeped into the packet of Black Cats, and only one fuse ignited. It sputtered a few times, then exploded with a weak pop . . . surely not loud enough to alert anyone at a distance. It was, however, loud enough to disturb a sensitive monkey. He ran to the north end of the island and squatted on the end of a log that had washed partially ashore.

"It's nice to know they're looking for us," said Emmet.

"That's better than nothing," Warren agreed.

Emmet looked at his new pal, who was muddy and wet from head to toe. "Warren, we've only been friends for three days, and already I've gotten us into a serious jam. You know, there's a chance we might not make it out of here alive. I hope you'll forgive me if that happens."

"It's not your fault, Emmet." Warren was diplomatic. "Sometimes you eat the bear, and sometimes the bear eats you."

"Yeah. Life is a gamble."

"Got to risk losing to win."

The philosophizing friends were suddenly distracted by the sound of Senator screeching at the top of his lungs. They ran to investigate, arriving in time to see the log and Senator cast free of the island and begin to drift downstream. Senator clung to a broken limb and cried for intervention. There was nothing the boys could do.

Emmet groaned, "He doesn't know how to swim."

The boys froze and watched in horror as the current carried the log toward a whirlpool south of the island. Senator's eyes grew to the size of silver dollars as his simple craft followed a straight line toward the turbulent water. He shut them tighter than a dime when he sailed into the outer periphery of the whirlpool and began to bob around it like a string toy. The boys couldn't see his eyes at all when the log abruptly disappeared beneath the choppy surface.

"Senator!" Emmet screamed. Then, quietly, "That's all she wrote."

"I'm sorry, buddy." Warren put an arm around Emmet.

Emmet sniffled. "I really loved that monkey. He was nicer than most people."

"Real polite," Warren agreed.

Suddenly they heard a loud *glug*, followed by a *whoosh*. The log shot from the water and flew ten feet in the air, flipping end over end before slapping down with a splash. It sat for but a second before the current drew it south. Clamped to the stub of the broken branch was a patch of brown fur. It was Senator. He signaled with his tail that he was alive.

The tears in Emmet's eyes began to sparkle. "Hallelujah!"

Warren jumped and cheered. "That little bugger sure is holding on tight!"

Click. A light bulb lit in Emmet's head as he watched Senator sail out of sight. He punched the air with a triumphant fist. "Warren, I've got it! We're going to build us a boat and sail off of this stinking, shrinking island."

69

"Now you're talking like a Yankee!" Warren cried.

"Okay. We've got maybe an hour of light," Emmet noted as he began to look around for suitable timber. "That gives us no time to lose."

It was about seven when Henry returned to Leopold's after traipsing through the lower reaches of the swamp for over an hour. What he'd seen there had turned him into a nervous wreck. Leopold and Garland tried to soothe him with hopeful words, but their efforts were in vain. Henry could not be reached with mere words. A dark force held him in a second world. Leopold knew the look. He determined it was time for spiritual fortification. He unlocked the corner cupboard and retrieved from the bottom shelf a one-gallon crock. "Here. Take a swig of this," he said in a reassuring tone as he uncorked the container and handed it to Henry. "Just a taste is all you'll need." He glanced knowingly at Garland as Henry put the jug to his lips. But Henry did not sip—he chugged.

Henry withdrew the jug from his lips and asked in a hoarse whisper, "What is this stuff?"

"Just a spot of homemade eau-de-vie I keep for emergencies," Leopold boasted. "It'll cure almost anything that ails ya."

"Wingdiggidy!" Henry huffed as the liquid went down.

"Wingdiggidy is right," Leopold smiled.

Flea skidded the station wagon into the yard just a moment after Henry had imbibed Leopold's cure-all. When Henry saw his wife and daughters get out of the car, he darted from the house to greet them. Before he reached the station wagon, he tripped over a bucket, flew eight feet, then landed on his backside in a garden wagon. The impact rolled the wagon two feet forward, which was just the distance needed to catapult it over the crest of an incline. "Whoa!" Henry hollered as the wagon gained speed and shot down the hill.

He was upside down, head pointed backward, and not quite sure what had hit him.

Clementine chased after her husband, popping over the crest of the hill in time to see the wagon barreling toward the floodwater. Wade Butcher leaped out of nowhere and toppled the runaway vehicle. Henry pitched free, tumbled over the soggy ground, and somehow bounced to his feet. Clementine rushed to him and threw her arms around his chest. "Henry, oh, Henry! What's happening here?" She hugged him hard.

"Don't know," Henry muttered honestly.

Suddenly, thirty yards from where Clementine and Henry were standing, Goosebumps began to bay like a champion hound. He stood haunch deep in the water and pointed at an incoming object. Wade Butcher ran to investigate. In the dwindling light he could see a log bobbing in the murky water. Atop the log, holding on with one foot and a tail, he could see Senator waving to him. "It's the monkey!" Wade shouted. "He's coming in."

And so Senator was safely returned to his clan. But what of his partner, Emmet, and the new kid, Warren?

It is impressive what two eleven-year-olds can accomplish when they set themselves to a task. The machete was a blur of motion in Emmet's hands as he whacked at trees, hacked at limbs, and sliced through small branches. Warren sounded like a warthog grunting in the underbrush as he pushed and pulled at muddy logs. The boys did not have time to draw a design for their craft. Instead they gathered anything that would float and incorporated it into a bulging mass. When the twine from the knapsack was depleted, they used vines and sinewy branches to weave the structure together. Somehow each understood what the other was trying to accomplish, and eventually the raft was complete. The builders then stepped back to admire a vessel in the shape of a **V**, about six feet long and two feet wide.

"What do ya say, mate? Think it'll float?" said Emmet.

"Absolutely, Captain."

"Mind if I give her a name?"

"Please do."

Emmet stepped forward and propped one foot on the jagged prow of their vessel. He bowed ceremoniously, then in a deep voice he proclaimed: "I hearby dub thee *Contessa*."

"What?"

"It's a girl's name. Ships are always named after girls."

"I know it's a girl's name. Why that one?"

"In honor of someone I met when the carnival passed through Binkerton last year. Her father has a monkey too."

"Aha. A gypsy girl?"

"No, a Baptist. But she was as cute as they come."

"Good for that. Now let's see what she'll do in the water."

The boys dragged *Contessa* into shallow water and climbed aboard. The idea was for Warren to ride the prow and deflect obstacles, while Emmet stood at the stern and steered with a pole. They never got past the idea. Once aboard, the current took the helm and *Contessa* began to birl out of control. "She floats!" Warren cheered. That she did, but her advance was made in a series of erratic spins and swoops. With every three rotations they progressed approximately a hundred yards south and fifty yards west. Here and there *Contessa* slowed as she dragged over reeds or a submerged bush. At one point she stopped completely. Emmet and Warren had to slip over the side and coach her through a patch of bramble. Once clear of that, she resumed her journey across the swamp with a more definite sense of direction. *Contessa* was being drawn toward the deep cavity of Polecat Creek, where the flood concentrated in a turbulent channel. As she neared the deep water, she gathered speed. Meanwhile the last light was falling from the sky.

The boys knew they were in trouble as soon as they felt the powerful tug of Polecat Creek. Faster and faster they went, until eventually they were swept into the main flow. It was too much for the hastily built craft. She creaked, groaned, and abruptly began to disintegrate. Emmet and Warren hit the deck, and in a frantic scramble they attempted to hold her together. They gasped for air as water rushed at their faces and tore sideways at their legs. What had once been a V shape was soon transformed into a sort of ★ shape. Desperately the boys clasped each other in a double wrist lock and held on for dear life.

It was a sullen group gathered around the small fire in Leopold's front yard. Garland Barlow stood in wooden silence like a totem pole, his arms crossed and a frown chiseled on his face. Wade Butcher sat chewing fingernails that no longer existed. Bellamonte Smoot leaned against a log and prayed. Flea Jenfries was skittish. She popped in and out of the flickering shadows like a hyperactive spy. Nearby a unit of volunteers huddled and discussed the possibilities. Clementine and Henry stood arm in arm, with Holly and Matilda nestled against them. They stared silently into the dark expanse of the unforgiving swamp and forced themselves to think positive thoughts.

Leopold and Archibald took Senator up to the house, where in a series of grunts, hand gestures, and squeals, the brave primate was able to inform Leopold that the boys were alive and safe on high ground. Leopold ran with the news. The group could hear him calling down the hill. "Emmet and Warren are temporarily marooned on a haven of dry land. They'll be fine. When the current abates, we'll put a motor on the boat and go get them," he explained.

"How do you know that?" Wade asked dubiously.

"From Senator," said Leopold, as though it should have been obvious to anyone.

"The monkey told you, huh?"

"Yes," Leopold replied. "We'll have them out in the morning or before, unless something unforeseen happens."

"Unforeseen?" Clementine turned. "What could be unforeseen?"

"Anything, Clementine. I mean . . . nothing." Leopold was saved from further embarrassment by the timely arrival of Archibald. He was weaving as he walked, and he was grinning from ear to ear.

"Say," Archibald burped. "What was in that jug?"

"Which jug?"

"The one . . . hic . . . excuse me . . . on the table."

"You didn't drink any of that, did you?" Henry asked.

"Just a . . . couple of swallows." Archibald blinked at his father, pirouetted twice, and floated softly to the ground. Before anyone could reach him, he was snoring.

Time is a tiger. It is an old owl sitting in a tree. Scientific studies have led some scholars to suggest it is never ending. Whatever its full extent, Clementine and Henry were stuck in the stuff as they stood by the dark swamp. All their hopes were focused on the exactly now. Neither knew what to expect next. Where were Emmet and Warren? There was no history, no future; only now. And now would not budge. Fortunately they were holding hands, or surely they would have despaired. The sweat they exchanged from palm to palm contained bioelectrical charges of hope. It helped them withstand the wait. Hope, studies have shown, is one of the few elements in the universe capable of conquering time.

Somewhere in the dark distance a bullfrog croaked.

Garland Barlow thought he was going to cry. He walked away from the light of the fire to stand hidden near the water's edge. But before he could get in a sniffle, he heard what he thought was a human voice. He cupped a hand behind an ear. Then he heard it again . . . a small voice in the night. "Here, ya'll! Come quick!" Garland shouted. "Bring flashlights. Over here."

There was a mad dash of yellow beams, followed by the glint of forty eyes peering into the swamp. They saw only black water and weeds.

"Where, Garland?"

"I'm not sure. I thought there." He pointed.

"Shhh!"

At first the group heard only the sound of their own breathing coupled with rushing water. Then out of the darkness there came a nearly inaudible mumble. Hope surged through the crowd.

"Emmet! Warren!" Clementine called. "Can you hear me?"

One long second passed before a weary voice replied, "Is that you, Mom?"

In the next instant there was so much shouting, hollering, singing, and squealing that it was impossible to discern who said what to whom.

eight

THE NEXT MORNING Emmet awoke to the sound of Warren's sniffling, snorting, and straining to breathe through a stuffy nose. When Emmet looked across the room, he saw his shipmate shivering in a cold sweat. He got up and threw a light blanket over Warren, then went downstairs to inform his mother that their visitor was ill.

At nine thirty Warren woke up and dragged himself into the bathroom, where he relieved himself, coughed congested matter from his chest, and drank three glasses of water. He returned to bed and slept feverishly for five hours. When he awoke again briefly, at two thirty, Holly was there to change his sheets and pillowcases. Ever since she had learned that his parents were dead, she had felt a compelling need to comfort and protect him. Now was the time. It was out with the Annie Oakley look and in with something à la Florence Nightingale. "I have taken charge of nursing you," she said to Warren as she punched a pillow back to life. "It's my duty as the oldest daughter. If there's anything you want, just ask. Your wishes shall be my commands."

"You are kind." Warren yawned and fell back to sleep.

Holly took her duty seriously. Had Warren been royalty convalescing at Hilltop Memorial Hospital, he would not have been better served. For all that day and into the evening, Holly rarely left his side. The next morning he had fresh-squeezed orange juice and strips of cinnamon toast. At noon it was honeyed tea and peaches. Every hour his forehead was swabbed with a cool, damp washcloth. Although Clementine periodically looked in on the patient, it was Holly who remained to bless his every sneeze.

By that afternoon, a Saturday, Warren had recovered to the point where he was almost ready to get out of bed. His nasal passages had cleared, and his temperature had dropped back to normal. By this time Holly was utterly exhausted. She kept yawning so much, she hardly noticed that Warren was feeling better. Clementine came and helped the sleepy nurse from her chair, then ushered her down the hall to her room. Holly took one look at the bed and dove into a twelve-hour sleep.

Henry decided that after the week he and Clementine had just lived through, they deserved to treat themselves to a meal and movie together in Binkerton, without the kids. Flea volunteered to watch over things. She was a competent healer. She would know what to do if Warren's condition worsened. Also she was strong willed, and knew, or supposedly knew, how to handle the children. She arrived at Dither Farm at six. Clementine and Henry were waiting in the yard. They were ready to go.

"What are ya'll going to see?" Flea asked.

"Whatever is playing."

"If it's good, we might sit through it twice," said Henry. "That is, if you don't mind us running a little late."

"No indeed. Stay a week for all I care," Flea chirped. "And don't worry about Warren. I'll keep an eye on him."

"Check on Holly, also. She went so long without sleep."

"I'll keep an eye on her, too." Flea smiled. "Not to worry. Go now and enjoy yourselves. Pretend like Binkerton is Paris."

Flea was one of those people without children who know that life with children has ups and downs, yet still imagine the experience is a mostly fun enterprise. Granted, some kids are sweet, and almost all are predisposed toward amusement, but there are times—such as when you are the responsible adult—when fun is actually folly. And folly is aggravating.

The folly kicked in at about seven o'clock when Archibald led Dan into the kitchen to eat a bowl of oats at the table.

"Archibald! What are you doing?" Flea stamped her foot. "Get that horse out of the house."

"What do you mean?" he asked innocently. "Dan always eats at the table. Doesn't he, Matilda?"

"As long as I can remember." Matilda nodded. "By the way, Flea, Dan is a pony, not a horse."

"I don't care if he's a Kentucky Derby winner. He is not allowed inside. Out! Out, out, out!" Flea barked, pointing toward the door.

"Yes, Flea." Archibald led Dan away from the table to the door. "Aw, look. You've hurt his feelings."

"You surprise me, Flea," Emmet in. "I always thought you liked animals."

"Poor Dan," Matilda moaned. "Holly has been neglecting him for two days, and now he's barred from the house. I sure hope he doesn't get depressed and eat all Mom's flowers again."

"You children better hope I don't get depressed and knock your heads together," warned Flea.

A little while after Dan had been returned to the barn where he belonged, Flea went upstairs to see if Warren was feeling any better. She did not like what she found. He had fallen back into a fevered sleep. When Flea went to wipe the sweat from his forehead, he moaned and mumbled some nonsense about flying over treetops. She lifted him into an upright position, put an aspirin in his mouth, then forced him to drink a glass of water. Gently she laid his head back on the pillow and turned to leave the room. At the door she heard him mumble something about Emma Bean.

While Flea was upstairs, Emmet, Matilda, and Archibald decided it would be hilarious to take off all their clothes and sit in the living room. They pretended it was an ordinary event. Emmet read a book, Matilda worked on an embroidery, and Archibald sketched in a notepad.

Flea almost laughed when she entered the room, but then caught herself and scowled. "What do you think you're doing?"

"Excuse me?" Emmet asked.

"We're just sitting here," Matilda said matter-of-factly.

"You're buck naked!" Flea shouted.

"Oh, this? Nude bathing," Archibald explained. "We always have air baths on Saturday night."

"You ought to join us, Flea. They say it's good for your circulation."

"Benjamin Franklin used to take one every night."

Flea puffed up to her full size and shouted: "If you don't get your clothes back on immediately, I'm going to get your blood circulating so fast you won't be able to sit down."

"Ah, Flea. Don't be a spoilsport," Archibald said.

"Move it!" Flea grabbed a yardstick from the sewing machine. Emmet and Matilda scampered. Archibald dared to linger.

"Three seconds." Flea raised the stick.

"Yes, ma'am. I'm going." Archibald skipped toward the door.

"Better hurry or I'll blister your butt." Flea jumped toward the naked culprit and welted him one for good measure.

Clementine and Henry arrived early at the theater and bought tickets for the feature, a little-known film entitled *One Fell Swoop*. Shot on a meager budget in Brooklyn, New York, it was the story of a group of Catholics who banded together to fight crime in their neighborhood. They called themselves Rome's Vigilantes. Their sworn enemy, a nefarious mobster named Squid Lagoon, lived on a million-dollar houseboat docked near the Statue of Liberty. Ten minutes into the film, Squid was seen lounging in a hot tub, sipping champagne with five buxom women at his side. Suddenly his party was interrupted by a messenger. At this point Henry leaned forward and shook his head in disbelief. He nudged Clementine with his elbow. "That's Marvin Jinks. I haven't seen him since the day we parted ways outside the park in New York."

"Shhh," Clementine whispered.

"That beats all. Marvin made a movie." Henry was amazed.

Marvin Jinks was in seven scenes. Although his character did not have a name, Marvin did have speaking parts in two scenes. In his first appearance he burst into Squid Lagoon's private pleasure apartment and blurted, "Sorry to bother you, boss. Those crusaders have Snellings surrounded in a bar on Hobart Street." Marvin's other speaking part came near the end of the movie. It occurred just as he and another expendable character were about to be executed and dumped into the Hudson. Marvin glared defiantly at the vigilantes and said, "I'm not afraid of dying. I just hate to do it around people as ugly as you."

Henry was fascinated by the film. He convinced Clementine to sit through it a second time.

The fun and games stopped abruptly at ten o'clock, when Flea reported that Warren's temperature had risen to a hundred and four degrees. (Poor Holly would awake the next day to learn that she had been unavailable when Warren needed her most.) Flea did not need to explain the seriousness of the situation; the kids realized it was dire. They looked to her for instruction. When she said fetch, they fetched. When she said hold this, they held that. Meanwhile Warren's temperature continued to hover around the critical mark. Flea forced him to drink several glasses of water, which seemed to sweat out of him as fast as it went in. She applied an ice pack to his forehead. It melted. She wrapped him in a wet towel. Steam rose from the cotton.

Flea felt the situation had reached the point where professional help was required. She ran from the room to call Dr. Roberts on the telephone. No one answered at his home or office. She considered getting in her car and driving to get Leopold Hillacre, but then decided it would be unwise to leave Warren for even ten minutes. So, not knowing what she could do, she rolled up her sleeves and bounded back up the steps to the bedroom. She was alarmed to find that in her short absence Warren had gone from bad to worse. He was sitting up now, with his arms wrapped around his chest like a mummy. The moaning had increased, and he had begun to rock backward and forward in the bed. Emmet stood beside him with a hand on his shoulder, but Warren seemed unaware that anyone was in the room. After a moment he stopped rocking and sat completely still. His eyes focused on something in the air in front of him, and his face froze in a mask. Then, abruptly, he fell back on the bed and raised his arms to protect himself from an imaginary attack.

"Hallucinations." Flea's voice cut through the frightened silence. "If we don't break his fever quickly, he could suffer some sort of amentia."

"Amentia?" Emmet said.

"Brain damage," Flea explained.

"Brain damage!" Matilda cried. "Flea, I'm scared."

"Don't be," Flea commanded. "Run out in the garden right now and grab me a handful of heartsease pansy."

"What? I'm not sure . . ."

"Johnny-jump-ups. By the garden gate." Flea rushed Matilda from the room, then grabbed Emmet and turned him to follow. "You, go to the kitchen and put the kettle on to boil."

"Yes, Flea." Emmet sprang into action.

Warren was quiet for the moment, but he continued to sweat profusely. Flea wiped his chest and head with a towel. She wished Clementine and Henry had picked a different night for the movies. When Matilda returned, Flea exchanged the towel for the pansies. In the next moment the kettle in the kitchen whistled. Flea ran down to the kitchen, where she hurriedly pulverized the flowers and threw them into a cooking pot. Then she added steaming water and stirred, allowing the mixture to steep for sixty seconds. When it was ready, she filled a teacup with the brew, crammed a clean towel into the hot pot, and counted to five. Before she could have counted to seven, she had the steaming towel in one hand, the teacup in the other, and was bounding up the stairs as fast as her skinny legs would go.

"He's starting to mumble weird stuff," Emmet informed her as she ran into the room. "I think he's delirious."

Flea handed Emmet the towel. "Rub his neck and back with this. I'm going to make him drink."

Warren looked right through Flea as she put the cup to his lips. She managed to pour some of the beverage into his mouth, but most of it dripped and drooled over his chin. The moaning, which had earlier been a mumble, now became a babble. It was as though he were speaking to someone or something far away. He repeated the names "Orville" and "Wilbur," and said the phrases "fly," "push," "shove," "up," "watch out," "pull," and "tug." Over and over he spoke the same selection of words. And there was a rhythm to his delivery, almost as if he were reciting a poem or a chant.

"He's got swamp fever and it's my fault," Emmet cried.

"He's having a psychotic episode," said Flea.

Matilda sat on the floor at the foot of Warren's bed. She was too frightened to be of any more assistance. Without thinking, she put pen to paper and wrote down the words Warren was ranting.

Since earlier in the evening, when Warren's condition had taken a turn from bad to worse, Archibald had been silent and withdrawn. A forgotten observer, he sat alone in a corner, hunched forward with his chin resting on balled fists, watching the drama around the sickbed. Now, with Warren trembling and spouting nonsense, and with Flea seemingly at wit's end, he leaped to his feet and approached the bed. "Stand back, Flea," he said. "Let me see what I can do."

"Archibald, this is no time for a prank."

"This is no prank, Flea. I have an idea. I want to try something Leopold taught me."

"What is it?"

"Just something Leopold told me about the night Emmet and Warren were in the swamp." Archibald shrugged. "It's just some words that he said could be used when someone was in shock."

"I don't know, Archibald."

"Please, Flea," Archibald pleaded. "Just one minute, let me try. I think it might help."

Flea could see that Archibald was serious. "Oh, go ahead," she assented. "Nothing else is working."

Archibald took a couple of deep breaths and sat on the bed so that he and Warren were face to face. He put a hand on each of Warren's shoulders and held him steady.

"Arch," Emmet whispered, "be careful."

"Shhh," Archibald ordered. "I'm trying to concentrate."

After inhaling and exhaling a few more times, Archibald jutted his big face to within an inch of Warren's nose. He grimaced and scrunched his eyebrows together, and stared into Warren's dilated pupils. Within a few seconds Warren's babbling decreased and he appeared to relax a little. Next Archibald jutted his face even closer and lightly tapped his forehead against Warren's. Then in a commanding voice he shouted: "*Hoche haumdoo! Hoche haumbee! Hoche, hoche, haumdoobee!*"

Whether it was by force of the words themselves or by the voluminous impact of Archibald's voice, or whether Flea's brew had begun to take effect, Warren responded with a blink of the eyes. He quit babbling, blinked again, and relaxed his shoulders. Tension drained from his body, and suddenly he reclined wearily on the pillow behind him.

Archibald studied Warren's face for a moment, then withdrew from the bedside. Flea stepped forward and placed her wrist on Warren's forehead. "The fever is broken," she announced, turning to Archibald with curious respect. "What did you do? Those words . . . what are they?"

"Leopold didn't tell me." Archibald shrugged again. "He just said it was some mumbo jumbo that he found in one of the old books he inherited from his father. But he said it might work."

"Well . . ." Flea started to say something, then allowed the thought to drift away. She looked at Warren and smiled. He was sleeping peacefully. She moved to Archibald and kissed him on his precious head.

PART THREE

nine

FOLLOWING WARREN'S rapid (some say miraculous) recovery, life, as much as it is ever a normal affair, returned to that state on Dither Farm. At least for a while.

During the next week or so, the only eventful news was Holly being asked to ride Dan at the head of the Fourth of July parade in Binkerton. She received the invitation in a letter from Eugenna White, the director of the Women's Auxiliary Branch of the Binkerton Volunteer Fire Department. As the letter said in bold print: **It is quite an honor to be selected.** No one needed to tell Holly. She sensed immediately it was the break she had been waiting for. She wrote back to Eugenna, "Dan and I will be delighted to take the lead."

Emmet and Warren entertained the idea of going back into Weeping Willow Swamp to find the bullfrogs, but they knew they were just fooling themselves. The notion of entering that muddy morass gave them shivers. They decided instead to build an addition onto Senator's tree house. It was a challenging project that temporarily satisfied their appetite for adventure. They had to scrounge the local dumps for construction materials and lug the supplies through the woods to the building site, where everything then had to hauled up the beech tree.

Matilda went on being the same redheaded Matilda she always was: that is, she continued to feed her intellect and exercise her imagination. She pored over the library books on oriental carpets, developing a fascination for both the rugs and the people who weave them. In her usual pragmatic style, she read every available reference on the subject. She learned how the wool was gathered, spun, and dyed, and how the carpets were meticulously created knot by hand-tied knot. She studied the designs that identified the places of origin of each carpet, and then located them on a world map.

Archibald spent many of his mornings sitting on a fence post watching his mother cultivate the garden. While she worked, they held a variety of conversations, tackling topics ranging from the intellectual life of an ant to the likelihood of life in outer space. Most afternoons he would meander to Aylor's Store and visit with Carl. Sometimes, when nothing else was going on, Carl would speak of his experiences at sea. He had been one of the Navy's best anti-aircraft gunners and was twice decorated for valor.

"Gosh, Carl, you tell it like it happened yesterday."

"Well, Arch, when you're out there, constantly surrounded by horizons, the details become etched in your mind forever."

"Wow. Those guys never stood a chance. Say, Carl, mind if I put a soda on your tab?"

"No indeed. Get some crackers, too, if you want."

Henry remained the productive farmer. He worked hard during the day, ate well in the evening, and was generally pretty wibberniffled at night. He was happy. Clementine was happy. And there was another one on the way. One lazy evening, Clementine gathered the children on the porch and made the announcement.

"I don't know if any of you have noticed," she said, patting her stomach, "but sometime around cider season you're going to have another sibling."

"Ah, Mom."

"That's wonderful."

"What's a sibling?"

"A baby, Archibald. Don't be so stupid."

"When in cider season?"

"By Thanksgiving, I hope."

"A boy or a girl?"

"Archibald, if your brain was the least bit smaller it would drop out of your nose."

"He's got a big nose."

"Congratulations, Mom. Good going."

"Can I name it?"

"No, Archibald. That is up to your father and me. But you're welcome to make suggestions, if you like."

"I'm going to do just that, Mom. I'll make a list."

Emma's first two weeks in Washington were busy ones. Her training curriculum was a big hit in the intelligence community. She taught two courses: Introduction to Sharp, and Trans-Sharp. Her classes were well attended, with ambitious agents competing for a limited number of learning slots. Applicants were accepted or rejected based on how Emma scored them on the admission exam. (She called it a submission exam.) Out of seventy individuals who filled out the questionnaire, twenty-five made the grade: twenty in the introductory course, and five in advanced training.

Those individuals who made the advanced class were given the chance to work with the Zandinski Box, a top-secret, low-tech instrument designed to enhance the inherent psychic powers that exist in every thinking human. The Box was invented in the late 1970s by Krol Zandinski, a scientist who worked as an independent reseacher in the field of parapsychology. The Box was the principal reason that Emma Bean was invited to Washington. Her contract specifically stated that she should train certain government employees in its use. After the unfortunate snowmmobile accident that took Krol's life, she was one of the few people in the world known to have mastered the instrument.

The Box was deceptively simple. It was four inches square. In the front was a round magnifying glass through which the user looked at an array of nine small mirrors that were fastened to the back wall.

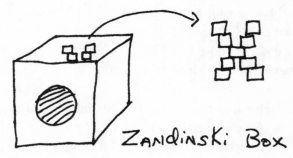

ZANdINSKi BOX

In the evenings Emma enjoyed herself. A slew of suitors (mostly sleuths) lined up to wine and dine her. It was her mind they were after. Not only did she have upward access, she also had a deft sense of humor—a rare commodity in the District of Columbia. From Capitol Hill to Dupont Circle, from Georgetown to Adams Morgan, night after night she was feted.

Yet (and this surprised Emma) despite the bright minds and flattering faces contending for her attention, she often caught herself thinking of Leopold Hillacre.

"What are you ruminating about, Miss Bean?" asked Simmons, the official sitting with her at the table in the Four Seasons. He was the liaison from the National Security Counsel to Emma's project. He was constantly at her side.

"Oh. A lepidopterist I recently became acquainted with."

"Excuse me?"

"A man with a long stride and a soft net."

"Yes, I see," said Simmons, though he had not a clue.

As for the man with the long stride and soft net, he was inspired when he heard how Archibald had used the *hoche haumdoo* chant to break Warren's fever. The incident reawakened the mystic within him and renewed his curiosity in all things hidden in the world. He was now determined to complete a project that he had begun some thirty years before: *The Comprehensive Guide*. From the shelves of his tremendous library he withdrew a variety of rare, leather-bound books left to him by his father, Winston Hillacre. He then proceeded, with open mind and passionate heart, to dive into the study of these esoteric texts. Some may think it a labor to leaf through thousands of pages of obscure, arcane writings on the tenuous subject of the higher spirit; but not Leopold. He had a knack. No detail was too small for his scrutinizing mind and no concept too large for his soul. He thrived on the hunt for subliminal messages and was especially adept at reading between the lines.

Once he got started, he found it difficult to stop. Day after day, nights afterward, sometimes for sixteen hours at a stretch, he attended to the yellowing pages and hungrily devoured their musty offerings. While he devoured, he copied, collated, cogitated, and reacquainted himself with his metaphysical Baedeker, *The Comprehensive Guide*. He arranged his notes into categories and compiled a glossary for acronyms, foreign phrases, and big words. Of course, given the obtuse nature of the work, only he could see where he was heading with it all.

As it is with many artists, philosophers, tinkerers, and thinkers, Leopold was so absorbed by his mental work that he hardly noticed the physical toll it was taking. The endless hours of bending over his lamp-lit worktable strained his back and eyes. Also, without his realizing it, these days and nights of deep thought were straining his brain.

Around noontime on June fifteenth, a Monday, Matilda, Archibald, and Goosebumps hiked to Leopold's house and rapped at his door. When the elderly eccentric poked his head outside and addressed the youngsters, it was the first time in a week that he had verbalized his thoughts. Consequently his voice squeaked a couple of times before it found its range. "Hiya. MatilDA. ArCHIbald. You bring me GOOSEbumps. Hello."

"Hi, Leopold. How are you?" inquired Matilda.

"Yes, very much. I'm fine. Come in, come in." Leopold held open the door. "What brings you to visit?"

"We need your help figuring out something."

"It's complicated stuff," said Archibald.

"Then you've come to the right place." Leopold smiled. "Complicated stuff seems to be my specialty these days. What is it you want to know?"

"It has to do with Warren and the *hoche haumdoo* chant, and maybe Aunt Emma," said Matilda. "I think something spooky is going on."

"Spooky?" asked Leopold.

Matilda rolled her eyes. "Mysterious, anyway."

"Okay. It's not spooky, but it is mysterious. And you say it involves Warren and the chant."

"Yes," said Matilda.

"And your aunt Emma."

"And her."

"Hmmm." Leopold rubbed his chin. "That does sound serious."

"It is," said Archibald.

"Well, in that case, follow me." Leopold led his visitors toward the west wing of the house. It was an area where the children had never been. Usually this side of the house was shut off by thick double doors. But today they were swung open. Matilda and Archibald were thrilled. They had often wondered what secrets were to be found in the west wing of the Hillacre estate.

Leopold guided the children through a narrow, dimly lit corridor with walnut floors and rough plastered walls. Some colored light entered the hall through overhead stained-glass windows, but it was hardly enough to pitch a shadow. Out of nervousness and excitement, Matilda reached for Archibald's hand. He looked askance at her, but did not draw away. At the end of the hallway was a six-sided mahogany door with a brass knob. Above the knob was an oval-shaped, bubble-glass window.

"Looks like a hatch for a wooden submarine." Archibald pulled free of his sister and crossed his arms.

"It's shaped like a honeycomb cell," noted Matilda.

"Yes. It does. It is," Leopold agreed on both counts. "My father bought it in New York, in 1901, from a Prussian fellow who was down on his luck. He strapped it to the roof of his buggy and hauled it here himself."

"He must have looked pretty weird crossing Virginia with that thing," Archibald said.

"Well, he looked a bit weird anyway." Leopold twisted the brass knob and pushed open the door. "Welcome to my Inner Sanctum. This is where I work on complicated stuff."

The visitors trod softly as they followed Leopold into the spacious Inner Sanctum. Sixty feet long and forty feet wide, with a twenty-two-foot cathedral ceiling, it was the size of a small gymnasium and almost as cluttered as Aylor's Store. At the far end of the room were a massive black-marble fireplace and above it a chestnut mantel, upon which a stuffed fox and a stuffed wolverine eyed each other cautiously. Lining the walls were specimen cabinets, display cases, storage shelves, bookshelves, shuttered insets, old oil paintings, maps, and faded photographs. The center of the room was dominated by a huge oak table decorated with teacups, books, papers, pencils, protractors, prisms, magnifying glasses, and other implements of philosophy.

Matilda looked down. Scattered over the floor were more than a dozen antique oriental carpets. Archibald craned his neck and looked up. Hanging in the open ceiling was a prototype for a pedal-powered flap-wing flying machine. Goosebumps raised the hair on his haunches and stared straight ahead. He wanted to be ready if the fox or the wolverine made a move.

"A museum," Archibald whispered in awe.

"A mosque," Matilda uttered reverently.

"Feel free to look around," said Leopold. "And relax. That's the rule in the Inner Sanctum."

Matilda glided across the floor to a large carpet that had grabbed her attention. It was a deep-red color with white, blue, and ivory floral designs spreading from the center. It had broad borders divided into narrow strips by conventionalized domes interspersed with octagonal shapes. The design suggested to Matilda that the carpet was woven in Turkestan. A Sehna knot pattern and the use of camel and goat hair in the wool supported her theory. She guessed: "Is this a Tekke-Turkoman?"

"Matilda! I didn't know you were a carpet connoisseur."

"Am I right?"

"Not quite. It's a Pende from the Merv Oasis. But my father bought it from a dealer who thought it was a Tekke-Turkoman."

"It's beautiful."

"It is that. But . . . well, come look at this." Leopold shuffled over to a corner and tapped his toe on a small brown-and-green carpet. "My favorite."

Matilda knelt to inspect the rug. The weft was wool and the warp was cotton. The central field was set with a tulip design rising from a dark-green background. The green was contained by a brown-and-blue inner border, outside of which were yellow- and sand-colored gulls. The outer edge and fringes were beige. "It's a prayer rug, isn't it?" Matilda asked.

"Yes. From Turkey. It's a Ladik. Very rare. But Matilda, how is it that you know so much about oriental carpets?"

"Great-Aunt Emma got me interested. She had one with her when she got to the farm. And then I did some research at the library in Binkerton. There wasn't much there."

"Your aunt Emma." Leopold put a hand to his chin and paused for a long moment before adding, "She certainly is an interesting woman. I wish I'd had more time to speak with her."

"Hey, Leopold," Archibald interrupted. He was pointing upward. "Does that thing fly?"

"No, Archibald. It's just a model. I built it from one of Leonardo da Vinci's drawings."

"What do you do with it?"

"I look at it, that's all." Leopold shrugged. "Sometimes it inspires me to think."

"Aren't you afraid it might fall one day and smush you?"

"No. It's up there with heavy wire."

"Oh." Archibald considered a moment before offering, "So say, if you ever want to take it down and dust if off, give me a call. I'd be glad to help for nothing."

"I'll keep you in mind," chuckled Leopold.

The two kids drifted around the room for another twenty minutes, gawking at the contents of the various display cases and specimen cabinets. When they were finished with their inspection, they joined Leopold at the center table. Goosebumps lay underneath with his paws crossed. He had one eye shut, the other open. He kept the open eye aimed at the creatures on the mantel. He surely knew the fox and the wolverine had been to a taxidermist, but he had the blood of a bluetick hound running through his veins and was not taking any chances.

"So. What is this mysterious, complicated problem you have?" Leopold asked his guests.

"It's not actually a problem," Matilda corrected.

"All right then . . . whatever. You do have a question, don't you?" Leopold rephrased his query.

"Yes and no. What we have is an assortment of curious facts. We aren't sure what to make of them," explained Matilda.

"What are these facts?"

"They aren't facts, exactly. At least they weren't very interesting until Archibald and I started putting them together."

"Go ahead and tell him," urged Archibald.

"Give me a second." Matilda looked crossly at her brother. "I don't want to lose Leopold before I get started. This isn't the easiest thing in the world to follow, you know."

"Ready when you are." Leopold ruffled his white crown and leaned back in his chair.

"Okay. Now. Let me see . . ." Matilda began to lay out her collection of curious facts. She started with Warren arriving sleepy-eyed at the farm gate. She told how later, when asked, Warren could not recall the mode of travel by which he had come from New Hampshire to Dither Farm. She then described Warren's strange behavior at the time of his high fever. She detailed the process by which he had begun to hallucinate and babble deliriously. She told Leopold about the glazed look in Warren's eyes and the zombielike expression on his face. She withdrew the sheet of paper upon which she had written his garbled words, and handed it to Leopold. For effect, she imitated the singsong manner of Warren's fevered speech. Leopold cocked an ear to listen while his eyes studied the paper. Matilda concluded her presentation, "Maybe you had to be there, but something very strange was going on."

Leopold leaned back in his easy chair and rubbed the bridge of his long nose. For a moment Matilda was afraid she had upset him by not mentioning the *hoche haumdoo* chant. Then he slowly lifted his hand away from his face and fixed a gaze upon the two children. It was a steady, intense gaze—almost a glare. A full minute passed without so much as a flicker or a flinch in the old man's face. Just when the kids had begun to suspect that he was caught in a trance, he rustled the paper and addressed them in a deep, serious voice: "You may have something here. I'll need a few days to analyze it. Come see me again on Saturday."

ten

WELL INTO THE NIGHT on Friday, after two hours of Parcheesi and forty minutes of Fish, the children gave up their pursuit of fun and went to bed. Their departure left Clementine and Henry alone in the living room. Henry's attention was absorbed by the wooden giraffe he was whittling for Emmet's upcoming birthday, at the end of summer. He was having difficulty proportioning the legs to the torso. At one point he considered snapping off the front legs and declaring his creation an ostrich. Ultimately he kept with the giraffe. Clementine was reading the list Archibald had given her earlier in the week. At the top of the page, on the left, he had written: *In the case of a girl*. And on the right: *In the case of a boy*. There were eight girl names: Rose, Lulu, Sally, Binky, Meg, Peanut, Pokey, and Sunflower. There were ten boy names: Vernon, Otis, Carl, Apple, Hubert, Wenzel, Casper, Potter, Milton, and Sandy. Clementine thought for a while, then put a check beside Wenzel. None of the girl names struck her fancy.

Holly sprang out of bed on Saturday morning with the pressing knowledge that in just two weeks she would be riding point in the Binkerton parade. In her mind it was definitely the star spot. The only other position worth noticing, she supposed, was on the firemen's float, which carried the Pageant Princess. People always made a big fuss over the Princess. Holly thought it was absurd.

The Binkerton parade started out small, in 1955, one week after the buildings along Main Street had burned to the ground. The parade had been planned and announced two months before the fire, which of course took everyone by surprise. (Theories still abound as to the cause. Eugenna White even published a book on the subject.) The organizers, in shock over the loss of their town, never thought to formally cancel the festivities. Again they were taken by surprise, only this time by a good one. On the appointed date, hundreds of civic-minded folks drove to Binkerton from the surrounding towns and lined the charred streets in a support rally. The townspeople, scrambling at the last minute to go ahead with their plans, mustered together a spirited, albeit scrawny, ragtag procession and marched proudly past the cheering throngs. Those who could contributed generously to the young girls carrying collection baskets. It was the start of something new. From this humble beginning grew the event now known as the Binkerton Independence Festival, or BIF for short. It was renowned clear across the Tidewater region and beyond. After two days of sporting events, agricultural exhibits, culinary competitions, and domestic-craft sales, the spectacle culminated in Binkerton's grand Fourth of July parade.

All of this was in the back of Holly's mind as she saddled Dan and cantered off on a warm-up ride to Aylor's Store and back. As she rode through the countryside, she imagined the brass sounds of the Binkerton Merchants Association Band following her along the parade route. The drums drove the horns into a crescendo, and the music competed with the roar of the crowd greeting her. She nodded and pranced forth. Close behind, she could hear the clopping of the other ponies and horses (drab plow animals compared to Dan) as they whinnied and followed in orderly fashion. Behind them, she knew, the majorettes tossed and twirled batons. On their heels followed the antique cars, which preceded the first in a line of colorful floats. This was her moment. She held her head high as she and Dan trotted past Aylor's Store, then turned and started for home. Two weeks! She could feel the love and attention pouring in already.

On her way home Holly happened upon Matilda, Archibald, and Goosebumps. They were marching in the opposite direction, en route to visit Leopold. "Why are you going there?" she asked.

"You wouldn't be interested," answered Matilda.

"Probably not," Holly agreed. "So what are Emmet and Warren up to? Did either of you notice?"

"The same thing they've been up to all week," Archibald told her. "They're putting an addition onto Senator's house."

"Boys," Holly sighed in exasperation. Then she signaled Dan with a toe and he burst into a gallop for home.

Henry was on his way over to Garland Barlow's to have some welding done when he saw Millie Ross's car pulled off to the side of the road. Millie stood outside the car, looking down at a flat front tire. Although Millie was a smart and attractive woman (indisputably one of the prettiest girls ever to hail from Willow County), she had never married. Some folks whispered it was because she had never found anyone good enough for her. Others said it had to do with her zany disposition. At any rate, here she stood stranded by the side of the road. Henry pulled over and stepped out of his truck.

"Hello, Millie. What seems to be the problem?"

"Henry Dither. Your timing is ideal. I was hoping someone like you would come along."

"Ah. I see. You got a flat. No problem."

100

Henry retrieved the jack and a spare tire from Millie's trunk and proceeded to change her deflated tire. He was just a little self-conscious. She stood so close behind him, he could smell her perfume. A job he could usually do in five minutes took ten. When he was done, he smiled shyly, grabbed the flat tire and the jack, and placed them in the trunk.

"One more favor, Henry . . . if you would." Millie nodded toward the woods. "My hubcap popped off when my tire went. Would you be a sweetheart and help me find it?"

"Of course. It couldn't have gone far."

They stepped over the ditch together and began looking in the weeds and undergrowth. Henry quickly spotted the hubcap wedged in a bush. As he was reaching for it, he heard Millie cry out: "Ohoo! Ow! I think I've twisted my ankle." She stumbled and caught hold of a small tree for support, cringing in evident discomfort.

"Let me help you." Henry rushed to her and put his arms around her waist. She put an arm over his shoulder and leaned against him. "Gently now," Henry advised. "Let's see if we can make it to the car."

"Thanks," she said, and laid her head on his shoulder.

As they emerged from the woods and were about to negotiate the ditch, a car approached from the south. A blue car. A station wagon. It was Flea Jenfries and Bellamonte Smoot on their way to the farmers' market. Henry looked up as they drove past. It took him a second to register their expressions. Then it struck him that he and Millie Ross looked pretty suspect coming out of the woods together.

Meanwhile, employing all shortcuts and walking at a steady pace, it took Matilda, Archibald, and Goosebumps just under an hour to reach Leopold's house. They were breathing hard by the time they arrived at his front porch. Matilda ascended the three steps and rapped on the door with her fist. They waited for a moment; there was no response. She rapped a second time, with substantial oomph. Again, no response. Archibald stepped up beside her and yanked at a leather string that was attached to a brass bell. The clanging reverberated in their ears, but even then no one responded. The house was silent.

Archibald jumped down from the top step and worked his way behind several bushes, hoping to peek through the kitchen window. Leopold often whiled away the hours there. Just as Archibald was gaining a good grip on the windowsill, Matilda, who had gone in the other direction, called, "Hey, Arch. Listen."

"What?" Archibald cupped his ear and turned toward the distant swamp.

"No. Come here. That way." Matilda pointed to where the porch extended around the side of the house.

Archibald cocked his head sideways and concentrated. "Yeah. Yeah, I hear it. Let's go."

"All right, but don't wake him."

Goosebumps and the kids followed the snoring sound until they spotted Leopold's white hair rising from the end of a hammock strung between the side porch and a shade tree in the yard. From the end opposite his hair protruded two sock-clad feet, each of which exposed the main portion of a big toe. The sounds coming from the hammock testified that Leopold was in a deep, deep sleep. They also testified to the amazing variety of sounds found in nature. Matilda and Archibald were awestruck. Leopold's exhalations seemed to issue from another world. His snore was a symphony, the sound of which is best described as a syncopated series of rich, bronchial snorts intermittently punctuated by high-pitched nasal wheezes rising from a droning consonance of rumbling, soft-palate sputters. Any jazz composer worth beans would have been envious of Leopold's harmonic resolutions.

In whispered tones, the children discussed the notion of waking Leopold and telling him they were there. They knew it was not the polite thing to do, but they had walked all this way and were anxious to learn what he had discovered. Archibald offered an ingenious proposal. "I say we wake him, only let's make it look like an accident."

"Excellent idea. But let me do it," said Matilda. She did not have to look far for the means. Spread out on a table next to the hammock was a collection of insect wings that Leopold had set out to dry. She selected a sturdy dragonfly wing and used it to tickle the hairs on top of Leopold's ears. She brushed them lightly back and forth, then stepped aside. He did not stir. His snoring retained its lyrical song. Matilda approached again and moved the wing crisscross under his chin. Still no response. She swished it across his neck, twirled it over his Adam's apple, and brushed it upon his lips. Yet still he slept deeply.

"Here. Let me show you." Archibald took the wing from his sister and pulled a chair up to the hammock. He stood on the seat and bent forward, tilting his head until he had a clear view up Leopold's nostrils. After winking at Matilda and whispering, "Watch this," he inserted the wing inside the left nostril and gave it a quick spin between his thumb and forefinger. That did the trick. Leopold exhaled sharply, causing the gossamer wing to whistle. The shrill noise startled Archibald, and he fell sideways into the hammock.

Leopold was jostled awake. There was an odd look in his eye as he sat up and muttered, "Archibald?"

"Hey, Leopold. How are you?"

At the same time Archibald was untangling himself from Leopold and climbing from the hammock, his father was on the other side of the county, climbing down into a funk. He was so unnerved after being seen exiting the woods with Millie Ross, he had driven three miles past the turn to Garland Barlow's welding shop before he remembered his intended destination. He did not bother to turn around. He had begun to worry so much, he was thinking out loud.

"No use dealing with a broken plow now. Between Flea and Bella-monte, Clementine is sure to get the wrong idea. And if that happens, I might as well keep going west."

For some reason it never occurred to Henry to go home and clear himself with Clementine before the damage was done. He just kept driving . . . until eventually he realized that his truck had pulled itself into the gravel lot outside the Hot Spot in Binkerton. Acquiescing to the moment, he parked and went in for a nip to calm his nerves. The place had changed hands a couple of times since he was a teenager, but basically it was the same old snake pit it had always been.

Henry sat down at an unoccupied end of the bar and asked the bartender for a shot of rye. At the other end of the bar sat three unkempt, spiteful-looking fellows. The younger and smaller two were obviously brothers. At a glance one could see they had been reared in ignorance and squalor. Yet they were charming next to the third fellow. He was blockheaded, smarmy, oily, and ugly. Henry tried to ignore the presence of the three men and think about his own predicament, but the sheer unattractiveness of the trio made him curious. Between sips he shot darting glances at the men. Each time he looked, the big, ugly fellow appeared uglier and more despicable than before. Eventually the brute caught Henry's eye and laughed. Then, with evident disdain, he gobbled a pickled pig's-foot, chased it down with beer, slid off his bar stool, and strutted over to Henry. His breath fouled the air as he spoke. "Ain't you the lucky fellow that married that oldest Gooden girl from over around Aylor's Store?"

"Maybe. Maybe not. Who's asking?"

"Crowley Hogget. And these two handsome boys is my nephews, Acorn and Bart."

Henry remained impassive. He motioned with a nod for the bartender to pour him another rye.

104

"She's a cute little thing," Crowley had the temerity to say just as Henry put the whiskey to his lips.

Henry calmly and deliberately placed the shot glass back on the bar and shifted his weight so as to face his antagonist. In a steady voice he informed Crowley: "My wife is not a thing. You are a thing. A miserable, good-for-nothing, worthless thing."

This time Henry was ready. He had been farming for twelve of the fourteen years since the occasion of his first brief brawl in the Hot Spot. Now he was a man. And now his dander was riled. Although he finally did hit the pavement with a thud, it took Crowley, his two nephews, and the bartender twenty minutes to toss him.

Leopold sat up in the hammock and rubbed his face until he was wide awake. He rolled his head and found himself eye to eye with Matilda and Archibald. Goosebumps sat beneath the table.

"Well. Here we are," Matilda said with alacrity.

"Yes. Yes, you are," Leopold observed.

"So what did you figure?" asked Matilda.

"Yeah. What's the scoop?" asked Archibald.

"Figure. Hmmm. The scoop? Let me see. I, ah, have been doing a lot of figuring lately. Give me a jog there . . . refresh my memory, if you would. What did you want to know?"

"About Warren, Leopold," said Matilda. "Remember we told you those facts and gave you a sheet of paper with words on it?"

"And you said come back on Saturday," Archibald added.

"Oh, yes. Of course." Leopold's face lit with recollection. "I looked into it that very evening. Sorry I forgot. Yes. That was before the digression got me."

"The what?"

"Digression; train of thought. You know, a detour. Anyway, after I finished with your conundrum, I began working some semantical puzzles—"

105

"What's a conundrum?"

"A riddle answered by a pun." Leopold lingered in thought. "Sort of. So, as I was saying, the puzzles I was working were in Sanskrit. I suppose that doesn't matter, really. Someday you will read about it in *The Comprehensive Guide*. The point is . . . one minute I was sitting there concentrating . . . and the next thing I knew, a rogue digression had hauled me off on a thirty-hour tangent! I just got to sleep here about an hour ago."

"We heard you cutting Z's," Archibald said.

"We won't keep you long," Matilda said. "You can go back to sleep as soon as you tell us what you figured out."

"Please, Leopold." Archibald clasped his hands in prayer and pretended to beg. "If you're not too tired."

"Matilda. Fetch me that notebook from the table." Leopold pointed with his nose. "It'll be a pleasure for me to show you what I have. Rather curious, actually. The compositional structure reminds me of a rune."

"A rune?"

"A rune is an Old Norse saying, or poem, often magical in content. You might think of it as an incantation. You know, a magic spell. Except I couldn't get this one to work."

"You tried it?" Matilda asked.

"I, ah, fiddled with it," Leopold admitted.

"Get the notebook," Archibald urged Matilda.

She handed the cloth-bound book to Leopold and stood waiting while he thumbed through the pages. Soon he found the one he was seeking. First he held it close to his face, then put it at a distance and squinted. Archibald leaned forward in anticipation, causing the hammock to sway. Leopold moved the notebook overhead and peered upward. Just as he was preparing to speak, a frog lodged in his throat. He coughed and swallowed.

"Want me to thump your chest?" Archibald offered.

"No. Thanks anyway," Leopold huffed.

"So what does it say?" Matilda asked anxiously.

"Ah, yes. Well, at first I thought Warren had been hypnotized, and that somehow when he got sick the fever dislodged the memory blocks that had been planted in his unconscious. But now I'm not sure what I believe. It could be just a nursery rhyme. It is very difficult to reason."

"Hypnotized?" Archibald screwed up his face in disbelief.

"So what does it say?" Matilda repeated.

Leopold eyed the persistent Matilda, implying with his glance that she should remember her manners. "Of course, this is merely my interpretation. It may not be accurate . . . especially considering the circumstances under which the information was gathered."

"Yes. We know that."

"Okay. It says:

> *Heads up, Wilbur. Look out below.*
> *Watch out, Orville. Here we go.*
> *Push, shove, pull, tug.*
> *Rise up, carpet. Get up, rug.*"

"Wow," said Matilda.

"Neat," said Archibald.

"Yes," agreed Leopold. "It is interesting."

Henry was halfway home from Binkerton when he began to feel the beating he had taken. With his tongue he counted four places where his lips were cracked. His left eye throbbed with pain, and there was dried blood caked on his cheek. His chest ached, his arms felt like lead, and he was aware of a boot-shaped bruise on his rear end. Yet the physical pain paled in significance next to the discomfort reigning in his mind. He was ashamed and embarrassed.

"Man, I'm so stupid!" he hollered out the window. "Why didn't I just go tell her in the first place? She would have listened. Now she'll think something really did happen with Millie."

When Henry got home, Clementine looked at him and logically surmised that he had been in an accident. "Henry, what happened?"

"It's nothing. I'm fine," he muttered.

"Nothing?"

"Not really to speak of."

"Henry—you're black and blue, there's blood all over your face and shirt, and you say nothing happened."

"It doesn't matter."

"HENRY. What happened to you? Why won't you tell me?"

"Nothing." He averted his eyes from hers.

"Then tell me nothing," Clementine said firmly.

"Okay. No big deal. It was her fault to begin with. She ought to know how to change a tire by now."

"Whose fault?"

"Millie Ross's. Didn't Flea and Bellamonte tell you about us?"

"I haven't seen Flea or Bellamonte. Henry, what are you talking about? What is this about you and Millie?"

"Nothing. Or hardly anything. It wasn't planned. Whew, Clementine, I'm so relieved. All this time I thought you had the wrong idea."

"Wrong idea! Henry . . ." Clementine stepped back and folded her arms. She studied her battered husband with a very critical stare. "Henry Dither. You have some explaining to do."

eleven

TO HENRY'S IMMENSE chagrin, Clementine listened to his tale without reacting one way or the other. Although she had complete trust in her husband, there was something unsettling about the idea of Millie Ross wrapping her arms around the man—regardless of the circumstances. She told Henry she needed a few days to think about things.

"Think about things?" Henry's mouth fell. "What is there to think about?"

"I'm not sure; that's what I intend to think about."

For the next several days Henry was kept in the doghouse. Clementine was not mean about it, but she was firm. It was not until the following Tuesday morning that she saw the humorous aspects of what had occurred. She was in the garden pulling weeds when she suddenly visualized the shocked expression on Henry's face as he spotted Flea and Bellamonte driving toward him. It was the look of an innocent victim. She knew in her heart that Henry was more likely to jump into a raging fire than mess with another woman. (Millie Ross later informed Clementine that Henry was so rattled, he dropped her and the hubcap into the ditch.) It was too funny. Clementine hurled a handful of weeds in the air and began to laugh hysterically.

Holly, who had been floating in a cloud of glorious anticipation for the 142 hours since she had learned she would ride point in the grand parade, happened to be standing at the kitchen window, looking out, when her mother tossed up the weeds and started snorting with glee. During the hours up until now Holly had sustained a mental image of herself as a stunt-riding cowgirl destined for the big top. She could hear fame calling to her from the future. Miss Holly Dither, Queen of the Saddle, a rising star in the field of equestrian entertainment. At night she fell asleep hearing the applause of delighted audiences. In her dreams she was the recipient of mass adoration. Even now, at the window, she was thinking, "Isn't life wonderful? Of course I'll make a cameo with Ringling Brothers." But then as Clementine threw the weeds up and flung her head back, Holly noticed the swell of her pregnancy. Deep instincts stirred inside Holly. All of a sudden she harbored feelings not related to stardom. She was reminded that she too was a woman who might one day be a mother. And with that thought, a door to her heart swung open and she fell from her glorious cloud. The door was a narrow one, marked "Warren." It admitted only those thoughts that flew on Cupid's wings.

It did not strike Holly as odd that her mother was rolling in the garden, convulsed with fits of laughter. What was odd was the overwhelming, compelling interest she had abruptly developed in the architectural plans for Senator's tree house. It dawned on her that the boys might need some help.

When she arrived at the beech tree, Senator was dangling fifty feet off the ground, by his tail, from a very flimsy branch. He was valiantly attempting to retrieve the hammer Emmet had just

110

dropped. It was wedged in a seemingly inaccessible fork between two small branches. Although Senator swung and stretched at length, he was unable to reach the desired tool.

"Hold it, little fellow. I've got an idea," Emmet called. He climbed down the tree to the limb from which Senator dangled, and began crawling toward the skinny end. The farther Emmet crawled, the farther the limb bent and the farther Senator could reach.

"Hey, Holly." Emmet looked down at his sister. "What are you, stupid? Don't stand under us."

"Why, do I make you nervous?"

"Scram," Emmet barked. In a mockery of obedience, Holly stepped one foot to her right. Emmet scowled at her and continued inching out on the branch. The limb continued to bend . . . until sure enough, Senator managed to hook a finger under the clawed head of the hammer. But just as he did, Emmet slipped sideways and fell from his precarious perch. Providence and luck limited his fall: Somehow he was caught and cradled in the branches of the limb below. Above, in a snap release of pressure, the branch whipped upward, propelling both Senator and the hammer into space. Demonstrating an agility that only a monkey knows, Senator somersaulted twice before landing beside Warren on the roof of the tree house.

The hammer meanwhile descended in a direct line toward Holly's nose. At the last instant she turned aside, and the hammer missed her by less than an inch. She was not at all ruffled. She bent and picked up the tool, turned her bright smile skyward toward the canopy of green, and called in a sweet voice: "Hello, Warren. You want to come and get it? Or should I bring it up?"

"Holly!" Emmet screamed in disbelief. "Didn't you notice that I almost got killed?"

"Yeah, I noticed. So, Warren, shall I come up?"

*   *   *

Matilda's mind had been working overtime since Saturday, when Leopold had shared his interpretation of Warren's sickbed chant. For three days she had been thinking nonstop, and now, while her mother was at home deciding to forgive her father, and her sister was in the woods pestering her older brother, she was on her way to ask Leopold a series of detailed questions. She was convinced that the saying was indeed a magic command. It had to be. And that is what she told him when he greeted her at the door. Although he would not come right out and admit it, she sensed he agreed. At least he took her seriously when she requested permission to experiment with his rugs.

> *"Heads up, Wilbur. Look out below.*
> *Watch out, Orville. Here we go.*
> *Push, shove, pull, tug.*
> *Rise up, carpet. Get up, rug."*

Matilda repeated the words for the umpteenth time as she sat on the small brown mat from Tanzania. She had high hopes for this particular carpet. It was the only one she and Leopold had not already tried twice.

Leopold expressed his growing doubt. "Matilda, I don't think it is going to fly. That chant is probably nothing more than a nursery rhyme you and I have never heard before. Most likely it is very popular in the New England states."

"Yeah, I shouldn't have been so hopeful. I don't know what got into me. I really did believe we were on to something."

"It's important to check these things out. Otherwise you never really know," Leopold said.

"I was really hoping . . ." Matilda's voice trailed off.

"Hope is human," Leopold said consolingly. "Some of us just have more of it than others."

Matilda's voice cracked at the edge of a cry. "After the *hoche haumdoo* chant worked for Archibald, I believed anything was possible. Now I feel like some dumb old fool. It was ridiculous for me to get so excited."

"It was not ridiculous, Matilda. Don't berate yourself. It is worth feeling foolish sometimes—especially if that's what you have to do to make discoveries." Leopold reached down, lifted her freckled chin with his index finger, and flared his nostrils at her until she smiled.

Later that same afternoon, a Tuesday, Henry sat alone on the hilltop where, fourteen years prior, he and Clementine had been married. He gazed over the pastoral lowlands with a melancholy eye. His thoughts were focused inward. He did not feel well; waiting for Clementine to think things over disagreed with his stomach. For the past three nights she had been doing what he called her "distance thing." She had slept beside him in bed, yet her soul had slept a thousand miles away. Although he knew he had done nothing wrong, he still blamed himself. Certainly Clementine was not to blame, he reasoned in a half-baked manner; it must be me. And so in this illogical state of mind he sat alone on the hilltop, looking without seeing. Hours passed, during which he descended deeper and deeper into a funk. Not even the shrill call of a sparrow hawk circling overhead interested him enough to look up.

Back at the farm, Clementine was increasingly aware that Henry had not returned to the house at his usual quitting time. She felt a pang of regret. She was eager to rectify the tension, to hold him in her arms and share with him the warmth of her forgiveness. He could act like a lump of coal sometimes, she thought, but inside he had a diamond for a heart. And although she did not approve of fighting and had severely reprimanded him for brawling in a bar, a part of her admired his spunk. "He can't help it if he's a man," she mused aloud. "I shouldn't criticize him so harshly just because sometimes he thinks like a mule."

As the afternoon melded into evening and Henry still had not returned, Clementine began to fret. She waited on the porch, twitching her naked toes and wondering if there was something she should do. After a while her thoughts were interrupted by the low rumble of Jimmy Aylor's hot rod approaching the house. She leaped from the porch and went to meet him in the yard.

"You're probably wondering where Henry is," Jimmy called from the car window as he eased in the choke.

"Yes. I've been wondering," admitted Clementine.

"Well, he's sitting up on Lovers' Knob. His truck has been parked by the path all afternoon. Hop in. I'll drive you."

"Thanks, Jimmy. I'd hate for him to sit up there all night."

"He'd do it too," Jimmy said as he leaned over and held open the passenger door.

Archibald acted quickly when he saw his mother leave with Jimmy Aylor. It was the opportunity he had been waiting for. He grabbed a cardboard box from the storage space under the stairs and ran outside to fill it with grass and dirt. Next he returned the box to the house and slid it under his cot in the pantry. Then he hurried to the barn and retrieved the garden snake he had captured earlier in the afternoon. He knew he was not allowed to have reptiles in the house, but no one had reminded him of that lately, and if he got caught with the snake, he planned to argue that he forgot.

After Clementine left with Jimmy Aylor to find her husband, Emmet and Warren took the checker set and went onto the front porch. They were pretty evenly matched. Warren won the first game. Emmet won the second. They were tied at three games apiece when Holly rode up on Dan. Both boys made an effort to be extra friendly. Earlier in the day Holly had earned their respect as a helper. Warren was especially impressed by her ability to cart lumber up the tree. "Hey, Holly," he welcomed her with a smile.

"Howdy." She tipped her hat, then swung her right leg in a smooth arc over Dan's head, dismounting with the agility of an acrobat. "We got a lot done today, didn't we?"

"Sure did. Thanks."

"My pleasure. So, Warren, I was thinking . . . if you have a hankering to ride Dan, now would be a good time."

"I'd like to, just as soon as Emmet and I finish this game."

"It's all right, Warren," said Emmet. "It can wait."

"Okay, later on." Warren hopped down from the porch and stood by Holly. "I'm not used to riding bareback."

"Oh, you aren't?" Holly blushed. "Then I guess we should probably double up. At least until Dan gets a feel for you."

"Fine." Warren nodded.

Holly jumped back on Dan and extended a hand to Warren. She scooted forward as he climbed up behind her. "You might want to put your arms around my waist," she said.

"Yep."

"Hold on now."

After returning in the afternoon from Leopold's house, Matilda had gone up to her bedroom to take a nap. She had been feeling let down by her failure with the carpets. When she awoke, her depression had lifted. Somehow she knew there really was a mystery, and that she was closer to solving it than she had earlier believed. She happened to glance out the window as Holly and Warren rode into the sunset on Dan. Her eye followed them as they went over the hill and disappeared under a bank of colorful clouds. The image reminded her of another evening. What was it? Clouds at sunset: pink, lavender, orange, and crimson. Hmmm. It took a moment, then—eureka! Matilda waved her pencil in the air. Now she remembered. She leaned over and scribbled: *Aunt Emma arrived at sunset. Sunset. Check with Leopold.*

*   *   *

115

Jimmy let Clementine off at the foot of the hill where Henry's pickup was parked, promising to drive back by in an hour to see if she needed a lift home or not. She thanked him, then turned up the main path leading to the high knoll. As she came out of the woods into the summit clearing, the darkness of night was beginning to settle over the grassy peak. Sitting there like a stone marker against the horizon, with his shoulders hunched forward and his chin upon his chest, was Henry. He was oblivious to all but his own thoughts. He did not hear his wife approaching. She came within a yard of him before she softly spoke. "Henry. It's me."

Henry rolled his head and looked sideways at Clementine. She seemed more beautiful than ever. He had always felt lucky to have her for a partner. Wincing as numerous sore muscles rebelled, he put a hand over his heart and started to rise. Clementine stopped him with a gesture, then moved to sit by his side.

"Honey," he said. "I've been up here thinking for hours, and I've decided there is nothing in this world I fear half as much as the thought of losing you."

"Henry." Clementine said his name like a prayer. When she rested her head on his shoulder her abundant hair fell over his chest.

He started to speak, then withheld the thought. Time had unleashed itself, and in doing so had formed a perfect moment. Except for their breathing, and an occasional sigh of contentment, they sat in silence and witnessed together the coming of night. When the stars appeared, they kissed. Neither she nor he was hindered by the cuts and bruises sustained during the brawl in Binkerton.

Long after everyone on Dither Farm had gone to sleep on Tuesday night, several miles away, at the Hillacre estate, Leopold was up working in his Inner Sanctum. At the moment he was trying to translate a Tibetan poem into Latin. He was having a difficult time. Repeatedly, just as he would begin to make progress, an unidentifiable thought would surface in the back of his mind and distract him from the work. Of particular irritation was his inability to determine the nature of the distraction, much less give it a name. Yet it persisted in vying for his attention every time he tried to concentrate. The ceaseless interruptions galled him to no end. He was forced to accept the futility of trying to work. With a grunt he shoved aside the translation, leaned back in his easy chair, propped his slippered feet on the worktable, and began seeking the source of whatever was nagging him. He had the unsettling notion of having forgotten something important.

But what? What have I forgotten? Something now, or something from a long time ago? Perhaps an echo from the bygone days of my youth. No. But where? Why now? This feeling that . . . oh baloney. Old man, you've been reading too much mystical mush.

Leopold had been working with his mind for over seventy years, and the idea of it playing tricks on him at this late date made him ornery. He adjusted a pillow behind his neck and looked up at the flap-wing flying machine.

I'll get this distraction. To catch it and inspect it is to cure it.

Leopold concentrated for hours. Each time he was on the verge of grasping the thought, it would inevitably fade and slip through his mental net. He knew it was there. He could feel it. So with the determination of a chained billy goat in love with a nearby nanny, he thought and thought, and struggled to be free. Indeed, he thought so strenuously that a snapping turtle on the bottom of Polecat Creek could feel him thinking. Yet whatever it was, the distracting thought would not come into focus.

On Wednesday morning as the sun rose, Leopold still had not divined the source of his distraction. It was time to admit defeat. He was exhausted. Responding to a physical need, he left the Inner Sanctum and went to the kitchen for a cup of tea. After waving his nose past the herb shelf, he selected a cinnamon blend. As he opened the box, the strong scent stimulated a memory deep within

117

his tired brain. First his cerebral cortex began to tingle, then a flash of energy shot through his medulla oblongata. Suddenly the thought he had been seeking jumped into his forebrain. He let it take shape, then pounced on it like a tiger. "Got it! Oh my," he exclaimed as he recognized the shape. It was none other than the face and figure of Emma Bean. He could see her as clearly as if she were standing in the kitchen. "Well, I'll be a goose egg," he laughed. "I'm not too old. I've been thinking about a woman this whole time!"

Wednesday began as a nerve-racking day for Archibald. He sensed trouble as soon as he awoke and looked in the box under the cot. His snake, whom he had named Fred, had escaped. How, or even why, he could not imagine. But Fred was gone, and Archibald knew without wondering that if anyone other than Emmet or Warren sighted the snake before he did, there would be trouble. Of course, he could claim he knew nothing about it, but given his past history, he realized it would be difficult to convince anyone of that. The thing to do was find the snake quickly.

Archibald got up and yanked on his favorite pair of red shorts, then sprang down on hands and knees to inspect the nooks and crannies in the pantry. It was the logical place to look. If I were a snake, he reasoned, I'd stay in here where there are flies and spiders, and stuff to eat.

In twenty minutes he had examined every square inch of the pantry floor. His efforts were not completely in vain; he did find a quarter and the corpse of a pet toad that had escaped several weeks earlier. But no snake. It did not make him happy to know that Fred was elsewhere in the house. Part of the challenge in finding him, he knew from experience, was to search without appearing to search. Otherwise he would be hampered by a bunch of tricky questions.

Sometimes it's tough being a kid.

twelve

ON FRIDAY OF THAT WEEK, eight days before the Binkerton parade, at about one in the afternoon, Emmet and Senator were sitting in the unfinished addition of the tree house with their legs dangling over the side. Neither felt like working. For the first time since his arrival on Dither Farm, Warren was spending the day apart from Emmet. He had accepted an invitation from Holly to go swimming in the river. The situation agreed with Senator. He was happy when he had Emmet all to himself. Yet Emmet was not in the best of moods. He had grown accustomed to Warren's companionship, and now he felt its lack. He was not jealous. Holly had extended the invitation to him as well. He was perturbed with himself because he was bored and did not know what to do.

Emmet began to think back to the days when it was just he and Senator, a loyal friend if there ever was one. It suddenly hit him that the little fellow had been real decent about accepting Warren into their world. He reached over and scratched Senator's furry stomach.

Senator was accommodating. He rolled onto his back and stretched outward. As Emmet's fingers raked across his rib cage, the happy primate twirled the tip of his tail and emitted joyful squeals. His affectionate display reminded Emmet of the other thing in life that Senator enjoyed as much as a tummy scratch. "Come on, you lazy varmint," Emmet said with a grin. "Time for a treat. Let's go to Aylor's Store and get some butterscotch ice cream."

Aylor's Store had been a going enterprise since the end of the Civil War, when the two-story frame building was erected. Five tremendous oak trees shaded the stone sidewalk leading from the gravel parking lot through the yard. A blanket of ancient moss grew on the north side of the trees, and there was a century of acorn remnants crunched into the cracks between the cobbles. The walk led to the porch entrance, above which was proudly displayed a hand-painted sign proclaiming: GET YOUR STAPLES AND MORE AT AYLOR'S STORE. The main chamber of the enterprise was a forty- by seventy-foot room with a high tongue-and-groove ceiling. In the front wall were two large plate-glass windows. The floor was oak. Oily with wear, it creaked in many places. Five aisles defined by three rows of wooden shelves extended in vertical lines from front to back. The walls on either side of the room supported additional shelves, as well as hooks for hanging articles. Everywhere there was something for sale: in barrels, in boxes, in the rafters, slipped beneath a bench, shoved behind a door. A team of ambitious anthropologists would have to work around the clock for a month to inventory the contents, and at that they would miss the merchandise in the basement of the Aylors' house and in the numerous sheds and storage buildings behind. Jimmy and Alice handled books, bolts, tractor parts, lawn mowers, food, fuel, fabric, seed, fertilizer, magazines, soft drinks, candy, furniture, tools, toys, nails, screws, sunglasses, motors, hats, belts, electrical sockets, socks, decorative items, fishing tackle, hoes, shovels, shirts, jackets, underwear, office supplies, special-order appliances, toiletries, guitar strings, and chess sets. Jimmy was proud of his commercial scope, and was not the least bit shy about reminding customers, "I've saved a lot of people a lot of trips to Binkerton and back."

Emmet and Senator arrived at the store at two thirty in the afternoon. Slow time. Jimmy had gone home to take a nap, leaving Carl to mind the register. All four hundred pounds of him sat behind the counter, taking up most of the space on the bus seat that had been installed there for his comfort. He nodded as Emmet swung open the screen door and entered with Senator on his back. "Hello, Carl. How's business?" Emmet saluted.

"All right, I reckon. Can't complain, not as long as the overhead fan is working. How ya been? Haven't headed back into the swamp looking for bullfrogs again, have you?"

"Naw. We've been working on the tree house."

Senator jumped from Emmet's back and scampered directly to the freezer. He bounded onto the glass top and peered covetously at the frozen offerings. Carl chuckled. "I hid the last container of butterscotch under the chicken potpies. I figured you two might be in this week."

"Thanks, Carl. You're a monkey's best friend." Emmet went to help Senator lift the heavy lid.

"Speaking of monkeys—remember that Cunningham fellow, the one who travels with the carnival sometimes?"

"Yes." Emmet snapped to attention. "I remember."

"He was through here just yesterday. I asked how his monkey was. Didn't have it with him, but said it was fine. He did say though he'd have it with him at the Binkerton Festival."

"Really?" Emmet tried to conceal his excitement. "He'll be there? Did he say for how many days?"

"All three, I reckon." Carl paused to recollect. "That's right. He mentioned he was running a charity booth."

Emmet and Senator consumed the butterscotch ice cream, then

121

lingered to visit with Carl. Emmet had to restrain himself from asking again about Mike Cunningham. He could not stop thinking about Mike's daughter, Contessa. When he and Senator finally left, they took the long route home. From Aylor's Store they walked by Nora Cook's luncheonette, then turned on the path leading past the Gooden place. He knew he ought to stop and say hey to his grandparents, but he did not. He preferred to dwell on the prospect of seeing Contessa at the festival the following week. At first he was ecstatic; the image of her dark eyes and perfect smile were clearly etched in his mind. She made him think mysterious thoughts. He realized that he was a complicated human being, full of surprise emotions. He basked for a moment in this new projection of himself as a mature person, then refocused his attention on Contessa. But this time as he called her image into his mind, his spirits, which had previously been soaring, sank. Suddenly he felt dejected and depressed. His thoughts withered and warped into worry.

What if Contessa did not remember him? What if he was but one in a stream of boys living along the carnival circuit? What if their moments together the previous summer were merely idle flirtation on her part? Had she been toying with him?

Doubts fed upon doubts. The next thing he knew, he was on the defensive. He wondered how he should react if she ignored him. Or better yet, he considered rejecting her before she had the opportunity to reject him.

Eventually Emmet caught himself and regained a modicum of emotional control. He felt ashamed of his own self. It dawned on him that being a mature, complicated person was not necessarily equivalent to being a happy one. Better wait until he saw her, he wisely determined.

If he saw her? Maybe she would not come to Binkerton. Maybe she was sick.

He caught himself again. "Heck with it." He picked up a stone, flung it at a tree, and confided in his pet. "I tell you, Senator, I'm in a mood over nothing. If I'm not careful, I might wind up living in a fantasy world like Holly. Or walking around wibberniffled like Dad."

This particular Friday in late June was a hot, sweltering day. Matilda, wanting to share her new fact, had been to visit Leopold again. Archibald and Goosebumps had gone with her. The visit had been a major disappointment. Now they were on their way back to Dither Farm, following an old logging trail that skirted the southern reaches of the swamp and led to a shallow crossing in the river. When they arrived at the ford, they waded in up to their knees, except for Goosebumps, who was up to his shoulders. Matilda spoke sourly about the visit. Again they had found Leopold snoozing in his hammock, but this time when they roused him, he was not at all friendly. Indeed, he was gruff. He said he did not want visitors, offering only a halfhearted, grumbling explanation that he was not in a frame of mind fit for the company of youngsters. When Matilda asked why, he dismissed the question with a wave of a hand. Then he pulled a pillow over his face and ignored them completely.

"He gave us the brush-off," Matilda said.

"What did Leopold mean when he said he was languishing?" asked Archibald.

"I think he meant his sides were hurting. Did you notice the way he had his arms wrapped around his chest?"

"I noticed." Archibald imitated Leopold.

"Whatever was wrong with him, we took a long walk for the sake of absolutely nothing."

"I don't know." Archibald grinned, leaned sideways, and flopped into the river. Goosebumps yapped and plunged in after him. Matilda waded across and sat in a sunny patch of grass on the opposite bank. She watched idly as her brother and Goosebumps frolicked in the shallow water.

Matilda's mind soon turned to the unsolved mystery of the chant. She regretted that she had not gotten the opportunity to tell Leopold about the sunset connection. She wondered if it was a piece to the puzzle, and if so, were other pieces also missing?

Archibald soon joined her on the grass. Goosebumps followed and shook the excess water from his coat. A light mist showered over Matilda. She was reclining on her elbows with her face pointed at the glaring sun. In seconds the mist warmed to beads of sweat. Archibald sat beside her with his legs crossed, picking at the mud and silt between his toes. Two crows flew overhead and alighted atop a humongous oak tree on the opposite bank. The smaller crow rotated his head and emitted a lengthy caw. It echoed along the river basin before gradually fading away. The larger crow eyed the smaller crow, hopped to a higher branch, and also emitted a caw. It was louder and more authoritative than the first. His caw reverberated for miles. When it subsided, a new dimension of quietude was added to the world. In the lull that followed, Matilda, Archibald, and Goosebumps could hear, heralding from some distant dale, the mellow lowing of an unseen cow. The moo was sweetened by contour and distance, and arrived at the sunny patch of grass sounding like a leprechaun's lullaby.

Matilda yawned and rolled on her side, where she had a backlit view of her brother. She noted how his profile threw exaggerated shadows onto the river. She was reminded that Archibald was not like most kids his age. He was more mature than the average seven-year-old boy, she thought, and though he was a joker at heart and took few things seriously, he was capable of participating intelligently in conversations at a level on par with teenagers. The trick, Matilda knew, was to convince him to be serious. She tried a scientific approach. "Archibald. I'm taking an important survey. You have to answer honestly. I want you to think about it first."

"Okey-dokey."

"The question is, do you believe in miracles?"

Archibald considered for a long moment. "Sort of I do, I think. It depends on what you call a miracle."

"Do you or don't you?"

"Some miracles, sure. I try to believe in everything."

Matilda frowned. The little crow said something to the big crow. "Do you believe in such a thing as a flying carpet?"

"Do *you?*"

"I did at one point. I'm not sure anymore."

"Matilda, you've been racking your brain over this thing since the moon was new. Fill me in on what you've got."

"The moon was new? What do you mean, the moon was new?"

"I mean when Great-Aunt Emma and Warren got here. It was the night of the new moon, remember? Dad said so, on the porch, when he was worried about Aunt Emma getting lost." Archibald snorted.

"The new moon . . ." Matilda's mouth fell open. "Archibald, that's it!"

"What are you talking about?"

"A missing piece! You just gave me another missing piece." She shifted her position. "Listen . . . first Great-Aunt Emma shows up at our gate with a carpet under her arm. At sunset. On the night of the new moon. Next Warren can't remember how he got here from New Hampshire. Then he goes into the swamp and catches the fever. This wears him down until he's delirious and starts mumbling words to what sounds like a magical chant. Even Leopold believed in it enough to help me experiment with his carpets. Okay, maybe nothing happened then . . . but now I've found two extra missing pieces: the sunset and the new moon. I bet they have something to do with the chant."

"Missing pieces?" Archibald asked.

"Yeah, you know, like to a puzzle. Critical facts," Matilda

explained. "Necessary ingredients. You have to have the right combination to make magic work. Who knows . . . maybe there are other pieces too."

"Like the rug Great-Aunt Emma was traveling with?" Archibald asked. "Would that be a piece?"

"Probably. But we'll never know. She took it with her to Washington—didn't she?" Matilda sat up.

Archibald released his legs from the lotus position and knelt on the grass. "Not to change the subject completely, but did I tell you that I found my snake yesterday?"

"What snake? I didn't know you had one."

"I did. A garden snake named Fred. But I lost him in the house. I had to search all over before I finally found him under Mom and Dad's bed."

"You know you're not supposed to go in there."

"I know I'm not. But then I'm not supposed to have snakes in the house either. Anyway, the point I wanted to get to is . . . I hope I can trust you to keep a secret."

"Of course you can trust me. I'm your sister."

"Okay. So . . . when I found Fred, he was curled up on top of Great-Aunt Emma's rug. It's been under the bed all along."

"Her rug! At home!" Matilda blurted excitedly, then calmed herself. "Are you sure it's the same one?"

"Looked like the one she had with her at the gate when she arrived. It's mostly gold colored, with blue and red along the edges."

Matilda shook her head in amazement. "Archibald . . . you are a genius. You just found *two* pieces—her rug and the new moon."

"I am kinda smart," Archibald said modestly.

"Incredible." Matilda flopped onto her back and began to think aloud. "Under the bed. Well, well . . . there we have it. Of course we can't be certain without testing it. Let's see . . . Warren got here almost a month ago . . . That'd make the new moon . . . *this coming Sunday*. But I don't know—we could get into a *lot* of serious trouble. No. We can't even consider the idea. Aunt Emma would be furious."

"Matilda." Archibald grinned. "I'm flying with you."

"Hey now. I didn't say . . . No. Don't jump to any conclusions, little brother."

"Not jumping," said Archibald. "Flying."

Meanwhile, one mile upriver from the sunny patch of grass where Archibald and Matilda were sitting, at a wide bend known as Flo Bottoms Hole, Holly, Warren, and eight other kids were playing a spirited game of Red Rover Over. Warren was a most impressive competitor. He quickly made a name for himself as a strong swimmer with an adroit talent for eluding whoever was It. Game after game only he remained free to run, twist, dive, and disappear beneath the surface. Often the combined efforts of nine other Its were required to capture him. Holly was proud to be his sponsor. She bragged to the fetching Holt sisters, Belinda and Jill: "Warren is a real dream, isn't he? But then of course, you wouldn't expect me to fall for some ordinary guy."

"We never know what to expect from you," Belinda said.

"Yeah, Holly. Warren is pretty cute, for a Yankee. But it doesn't exactly look like you've got him wrapped around your little finger," said Jill, the prettier, older sister.

"If you only knew," Holly said before plunging headfirst into the river.

Miles north of Flo Bottoms Hole, an oppressive heat wave combined with excessive exhaust fumes and made Washington, D.C., a very unpleasant place to be. Only those individuals sitting directly in front of air conditioners were remotely comfortable. Emma had the one in her hotel room going full blast. She had just received a memo notifying her of a meeting she was to attend the following Monday. Scheduled for noon, in the White House basement, she was to report on her program as well as give an update on the Zandinski Box. She doubted if anyone would appreciate her report. The memo listed the names of those who would attend the meeting. From the Pentagon was General Clay Batter, to be joined by his secretary, Major Sue Wright. From the National Security Council was Simmons. Representing the President was Bob Thrax. He would be accompanied by a staffer, Janet Libson. The CIA was sending Graves Copeland.

Emma was weary. She put down the memo, arose from her wingback chair, sauntered to the window, and pulled the curtains aside. As she studied a bend in the Potomac River where it flowed between Georgetown and Arlington, her eye was captivated by the play of shadows and light shimmering on the water. It reminded her of home. Washington had become too weighty for her delicate sensibilities, and she longed to return to her isolated cove in Iceland. As she contemplated these things, two athletes rowed around the bend in a scull. Emma observed their progress as they glided over the water, passing through the distorted orange reflection of the afternoon sun. She was struck by how much the boaters resembled two people flying at sunset on a magic carpet. She chuckled lightly, amused by the notion as she watched the scull recede from sight.

In due course her chuckling subsided. She began to wonder if by some wild chance— naw, impossible. No way anyone could figure out a thing like that. And yet . . .

When the phone rang, Emma ignored it.

thirteen

SUNDAY WAS ONE of those splendid, storybook days on which the blue sky and the green earth seem to have been painted by a wise, gentle artist. A light breeze held the temperatures comfortably below eighty in the open fields and downward to seventy-five in the shade. Throughout the upper stratosphere, suspended sporadically against the baby-blue backdrop, clusters of fluffy white cumulo-cirrus clouds floated past like gigantic popcorn puffs. The effect was spectacular. It was an ideal day for lying on your back and doing absolutely nothing. Or for those for whom the sky held no special appeal, it was also a superb day for tending to traditions and pleasant routines.

"Something is in the air," Flea said to Millie Ross as they sat down to Sunday lunch.

"Hmmm." Millie sniffed the cornbread.

"I meant in the air in general. You know . . ."

"Yes, of course," said Millie. "Please pass the butter."

Flea handed her pretty friend the butter dish and watched as she applied the yellow substance onto a square of cornbread. Flea waited until Millie seemed ready to listen, then continued, "I've recently detected the symptoms of love in five individuals."

"Have you?" replied Millie, suddenly interested.

"Indeed," said Flea in one of those happy voices that gossips get when they have something to share.

"Who?" asked Millie. She was always curious about love.

"For starters, Leopold Hillacre." Flea smiled at Millie's astonished stare. "It's true. I dropped in on him yesterday and found him daydreaming in the garden. He was wearing that worn-out old cape of his. Poor old coot—looked like one of the original bohemians."

"What makes you think he's in love?"

"It was written all over him. He wanted to know what I thought of Clementine's aunt Emma Bean. Of course I told him she was terrific. He liked that—said he thought so too. You could see right through him. I guarantee you he's pining for her as we speak."

Millie nodded. "I like Leopold. Who else?"

"The handsome Dither boy."

"Not Archibald!"

"No indeed—Emmet." Flea giggled. "I gave him and the monkey a ride on Friday afternoon. That sweet little heartthrob, he's been smitten by Mike Cunningham's daughter, from over in King County. Her name is Contessa. I've seen her before. She's cute."

"Good stock, those kids," Millie observed. "Go on. Who else has the symptoms?"

"Holly is in love," Flea continued. "The girl is flipped over Warren, the young fellow visiting from New Hampshire. She doesn't take any pains to hide the fact either."

"Nothing fickle about Holly," Millie said as she added a small serving of green beans to her plate.

"Very determined," agreed Flea. She paused long enough to pick a slice of cucumber from her salad.

"That's three, Flea."

"Yes." Flea paused again. It occurred to her that she might well be upsetting Millie with all this talk of romance. Love was something that had thus far eluded Millie, pretty and intelligent as she was.

"You said five," Millie prompted Flea. She was not upset; she was curious.

Flea chewed a mouthful of salad and swallowed. "Clementine and Henry are the other two. They have a love-buzz going between them that is so strong you can feel it across the room."

Millie pointed her fork at her diminutive friend. "Where have you been the last fifteen years?"

"I've been right here in Willow. You know that. What I'm saying is, they've fallen brand new in love. Started right over at the beginning. Juices are running through their veins like they were seventeen again. Clementine said so herself, though she hardly had to mention it. She looks like a pregnant teenager. And Henry, well, there's no describing him. The other day when I was visiting, Clementine sat on his lap, and I could have sworn he was going to recite poetry then and there."

While Millie and Flea were discussing matters, Clementine and Henry were at Dither Farm, loading the truck with picnic supplies. Their idea of doing nothing on a Sunday was to spend the afternoon at Sandy Beach, a picturesque swimming hole formed where the Mattaponi and Pamunkey River conjoin. A wide swath of sand, ample shade, and picnic tables made the spot a popular destination for families.

Clementine was not really concerned when Matilda asked for permission to stay home; Matilda often selected solitude over group activities. But when Archibald also expressed a desire to skip the outing, the mother in her became suspicious. It was not his style to remain behind. When she questioned him about it, he looked down, rubbed a big toe in the dirt, and explained, "Mom, I'm languished. I think I've got growing pains."

Clementine studied the innocent expression that appeared on Archibald's open face. She could usually tell when he was hiding something. "Hmmm," she considered.

"Please." Archibald hugged his chest as Leopold had done.

"Henry, what do you think?" Clementine asked.

"I don't know about growing pains, but it might be nice not to have to supervise him all day."

"All right, Archibald," Clementine said. "As long as you promise to be on your best behavior."

Archibald frowned as though he were offended by the mere suggestion of his misbehaving. "But of course, Mom."

Matilda spent many hours on Sunday wrestling with the dilemma of whether to trespass in her parents' room or not. She knew the carpet had been hidden because Aunt Emma wanted it hidden. It was not for her or Archibald—of that she was certain. Yet the temptation was strong. Today was the new moon. This was a once-in-a-life-time opportunity. Textile aviation! If it worked, the achievement would surely outweigh the crime. It was a matter of comparing the threat of punishment to the gain of actually flying a rug. "Ah, Goosebumps." Matilda laid her head on her hound dog's back. "If only I didn't have such a big conscience."

In the end she decided to ignore the consequences and act. At three P.M. she informed Archibald of her decision, instructing him to get the carpet and stash it in the hollow pine near the pond. Then he was to return to the house and wait with her until the rest of the family got home. (Matilda knew they would check on her and Archibald as soon as they arrived.) Afterward, they were to wander casually away from the house and rendezvous at the appointed tree at five minutes before sunset. "Be careful when you sneak off," Matilda advised. "Don't attract attention. We don't

132

want Holly or Emmet getting wind of what we're up to."

"Me? Attract attention?" Archibald was indignant. "I used to be a spy before I joined this family."

As Matilda and Archibald plotted their undertaking, Emma Bean was at the Hay Adams Hotel in downtown Washington, sipping tea with a group of foreign dignitaries. Her host was an Arabian prince named Fisal Mustafa. Also present at the table were Guy Lancaster, from England, and Hans von Gustaf, from Sweden. It was ostensibly a social brunch, but Emma had suspicions. She spotted Simmons, in disguise, sitting at a nearby table. She presumed he was there to ensure that she did not mention the Zandinski Box. She was miffed by his chronic distrust of everyone. Emma also felt uneasy about the waiter, who had an odd bulge under his jacket. She hoped there would be no gunplay.

Emma's uneasiness escalated. Although she could not put her finger on what it was that bothered her, she felt a distinct discomfort. She excused herself to go to the powder room. In the solitude of her retreat, she was able to concentrate. She had a vague premonition of sorts that something somewhere was not right. She left the ladies' room and hailed the concierge. He bowed politely and asked what he could do for her. She instructed him to inform her party that she was not feeling well and had returned to her hotel. Which is exactly what she did. (It may interest the reader to know that the bulge under the waiter's jacket was caused by a croissant he had snitched and was intending to eat as soon as he got the chance.) On the cab ride back to the Watergate, Emma realized that her foreboding feeling was not connected with the group at the Hay Adams. "This is weird," she thought. "What is it?"

She tried to let her mind float. It did, yet it produced no particular image . . . except for one fleeting picture of Matilda and Leopold standing together at sunrise.

Emma dismissed this as a sentimental projection.

133

Later that afternoon Matilda and Archibald sat on the garden fence and eyed the front gate for signs of an approaching vehicle. About an hour remained before sunset. Archibald was increasingly anxious. He was afraid the family would return late and prompt Matilda to postpone the mission. Already her resolve was wavering. He complained sourly, "I wonder what's keeping them. We never stayed this late at Sandy Beach when I got to go."

"Maybe it's fate," sighed Matilda.

"Or a flat tire," Archibald retorted.

"Fate can make a tire flat. Don't you know what fate is?"

"Sure. It's what happens."

"Yes," Matilda acknowledged. "Except fate happens for a reason. Otherwise it's not fate—it's just life."

"Fate, life, whatever. They're still late."

"If they don't come in time, I'll be sort of relieved," said Matilda. "I never liked the idea that it was a snake that led you to the carpet. The symbolism is wrong."

"What's wrong with a garden snake?"

"You've heard what the Bible says about Adam and Eve, haven't you?" Matilda asked rhetorically. "We already know we're doing something we've been forbidden to do. The snake is a symbol of temptation. We're supposed to resist it, not do what we know we are not supposed to."

"Phooey. Hogwash. Fred is a harmless little green garden snake. Just as nice as he can be. Probably the worst thing he ever did was eat a caterpillar."

"You don't get it, do you? It's so obvious."

"I get it, sister," Archibald said. "We are going to fly that rug!"

"Maybe." Matilda shrugged.

Archibald had no doubts. "Doesn't everybody get a chance to fly, Matilda. Besides, if that defenseless garden snake is such a bad symbol, then Warren must be a goat. We wouldn't be doing this without him. Or maybe Great-Aunt Emma is a witch. What do you say to that? Huh? Got any fancy answers? Or are you just chicken?"

Matilda was silent for a moment; then she nodded in the direction of the driveway and said, "I see a dust cloud. That's probably them now."

Matilda arrived at the tree with a full twenty minutes remaining before the sun was due to set. There was no sign of Archibald. She poked her head in the designated pine and looked for the rug. She wanted to examine it before Archibald arrived. But there was no rug in the hollow tree. She withdrew her head and searched around in the tall grass. She inspected the nearby bushes. Zilch. The carpet was not to be found. She poked her head back in the pine and looked again, this time more thoroughly. She withdrew from the hollow pine and screamed, "ArchiBALD! I'm going to wring your neck!"

Kicking at clumps of grass while she paced, Matilda waited for her brother with an anger that surged and threatened to explode. A wind was beginning to blow in from the east, and it ushered in with it a tower of billowing clouds that the sun had painted in lively pastels. Ascending toward heaven like canyon walls, the lofty summits were emblazoned with fiery red tops. A spectacular sunset was in the making.

Matilda was ready to erupt. She intended, when Archibald arrived, to do more than just chew his ear off. *If* he arrived. Hopefully in time.

There were four minutes left before the technical advent of sunset (according to that morning's newspaper) when Archibald emerged from the woods with the carpet slung casually over his shoulder. He was chewing a blade of grass and looked as though he hadn't a care in the world.

"Where have you been with that rug!" Matilda barked.

"Pipe down. I didn't want you leaving without me."

"Where was the rug?" Matilda's face was as red as her hair.

"In a safe place. No need to worry about it now. I'm here. The rug's here. Let's get going."

"Archibald, I wish we had time for me to skin your hide." Matilda shook a fist at her brother. "You lucked out this time. Now we have to get moving. Come on. Put the rug down in middle of that open space by the pond."

"Yes, Queen Sheeba," Archibald salaamed.

Matilda knew at a glance that the carpet on the ground before them was a masterpiece. As carpets go, it was small—sixty by forty inches, she guessed. It was obviously a tribal piece. Perhaps nineteenth century. The warp and weft were of goat hair and lamb's wool. The pile was a silk-and-cotton blend. It had a halachi design, with four main squares defined by a series of grazing horses. There was a woven dome atop the four squares, which suggested to Matilda that it was one of the rare engsi rugs she had read about. Certainly the knot pattern was dense enough, and the warm colors were definitely the product of aged vegetable dyes. Engsi or not, it was a museum piece that Archibald had taken from beneath their parents' bed. The idea frightened her. "I think we ought to put it back. It's too majestic for the likes of you and me," she told Archibald. "Besides, the wind is starting to pick up. It would be foolish for us to go up in these conditions."

Archibald tensed and stamped his foot. Then he snorted and stepped to within a nose-length of his sister. "It is our duty to try to fly this thing," he declared.

"Yeah, why is it our duty?" Matilda asked.

"Fate, big sister. Just like you explained to me. We aren't putting the rug back without giving it a try."

Matilda studied the clouds above. There was less than a minute remaining before the sun would touch the horizon. "And what are we going to do if it actually works?"

Archibald dropped the scowl from his face and grinned. "I don't know what you're going to do, but me—I'm going to hold on for dear life."

Matilda smiled. "You're right. We've come this far. You sit there, facing that way. I'll sit here in front of you and steer."

"How, ah . . . how do you steer?" Archibald inquired.

"I'm not sure. I hope all I have to do is watch where we're going and concentrate."

"You hope," Archibald muttered. "I wish I was a spy again."

If Leopold Hillacre had been there, he would have attempted to analyze what happened. He would have asked questions like these: Does belief cause the miracle, or does the miracle cause belief? Does energy follow thought, or do thoughts follow energy? Is there a limit to what the imagination can do? Is it possible to manifest fiction in our lives?

But Leopold was not by the pond. He was standing in the cupola atop his barn, taking in the sunset and thinking of things that might have been if only he had met a certain auburn-haired lady fifty years earlier.

Matilda exhaled sharply and sat down in front of Archibald. She flung her braids behind her. "In unison. Are you ready?"

"I think so. Are you?"

"As much as I'll ever be."

"Then go ahead. Start."

"Okay:

> *Heads up, Wilbur. Look out below.*
> *Watch out, Orville. Here we go.*
> *Push, shove, pull, tug.*
> *Rise up, carpet. Get up, rug."*

They waited. Nothing.

"Let's try it again."

They repeated the chant. Again there were no results. Meanwhile the sun continued dropping beneath the skyline. "Think," Matilda urged. "What are we doing wrong?"

Archibald scrunched his face into a thinking expression. Ten seconds later his eyebrows rose in victory. "Remember when Warren went bug-eyed and threw his hands up in the air?"

"Yeah?"

"Let's try that with the chant," he suggested.

"Okay. Ready, start:

Heads up, Wilbur. Look out below.
Watch out, Orville. Here we go.
Push, shove, pull, tug.
Rise up, carpet. Get up, rug.

"It's not work . . ." Matilda started to speak, but then her voice trailed off. There was the slightest pressure under the carpet. They felt it vibrate against their legs, and in the next instant they were rising up. Suddenly they were sailing over the treetops at a thrilling speed. Archibald called into the wind, "Matilda! You're thinking too fast. Slow down your thoughts."

"What? I can't hear you."

"You're thinking too fast," he repeated.

"Speak louder!" Matilda cried, turning her head to listen. As she did, the carpet tilted and veered to the left, nearly crashing into the top of a tall pine.

Archibald covered his eyes with both hands and hollered, "Watch where you're thinking!"

Matilda screamed. Her cry was gobbled by the wind.

In a matter of a very few minutes the astonished pair were several miles from Dither Farm. Having no particular destination in mind, Matilda's attention was focused directly ahead. They were flying southwest. Somehow, seemingly of its own accord, the carpet gained and maintained an altitude of about thirty feet over the tree-tops. The passengers were too frightened to consider making any more turns. At this stage they did exactly as Archibald had said he was going to do: They held on for dear life.

The wind whirred as it whipped past them. They could hear the carpet tassels fluttering. Matilda was afraid to look in any direction other than straight ahead. She sat like a statue, her eyes riveted on the horizon. Archibald was also afraid, but he did dare to peek once through his fingers. He shot a quick glance below, saw the land sliding beneath them in a blur of color, and closed his eyes again.

Before they knew what was happening, they were passing over the outskirts of Binkerton, flying in a southwesterly direction toward King County. The carpet seemed to have a mind of its own. Matilda looked directly ahead with wide-open eyes. She could hardly believe what she was seeing, much less figure out what to do. Eventually, though, she came to the frightening conclusion that they were following the setting sun. She realized that if she did not find a way to change their course, they might fly to California, or farther on, to Hawaii. She called back: "Prepare yourself. I have to try to turn us around. Otherwise we could wind up in China."

"China! Do something quick."

"Okay. One, two, three." Matilda slowly rotated her eyeballs and leaned to one side. The response was immediate. With a swooping motion the carpet tilted, banked into the clouds, and reversed direction. Both kids were amazed when they did not plummet to the earth. Somehow the carpet had remained beneath them as they turned. Somehow it had leveled off in an upright position. Matilda wanted to close her eyes and faint, but she was afraid of what might happen.

"I'M ALIVE!" Archibald opened his eyes.

"The centrifugal force held us on," Matilda hollered.

"I love being alive!" Archibald cheered, then added, "I've had enough flying for one day. What do you say we go home now?"

"That's where we're heading. I hope."

"Matilda. . ." Archibald leaned forward and shouted, ". . . how do you plan to land this thing?"

"Gently. I hope. Very gently."

Neither sibling spoke as they traveled east through the dwindling twilight, retracing their original flight path. As they flew past the outskirts of Binkerton, dusk had settled over much of the land and obscured many details. Even so, the airborne adventurers were able to recognize the farms below. Matilda grew more relaxed as a pilot. She had learned to expand her peripheral vision without causing the carpet to turn.

After a long two minutes, Matilda spotted the pine forest beside the pond on Dither Farm. Carefully, with stolen glances, she searched for the clear patch of ground. By now her breathing had almost stopped. They had to land, no matter what the outcome.

Archibald had discovered that it eased his trepidation if he pretended he was a duck. "Quack," he called.

Another minute . . . then Matilda saw the patch of open ground. With great concentration, she half-prayed and half-willed the carpet to land. Blood rushed to their heads as the rug dropped beneath them and descended in a free-fall toward terra firma.

"Quack!" screamed Archibald.

At the same time Archibald and Matilda were landing on Dither Farm, Leopold was climbing down from the cupola. He was confused. In the last moment of twilight he had seen, or thought he had seen, something streaking across the sky. It was just a speck—too far away to identify accurately—yet it was a very curious speck. He wondered if his mind was playing tricks on him. Probably, he told himself, it was just a couple of buzzards.

fourteen

It was happiness that hoisted Holly out of bed at seven on Monday morning. Only five and a half days remained before she would make her debut at the head of the Binkerton parade. She was back in her glorious cloud, held aloft by the memory of Sunday night. The scene, as she remembered it, had Warren bursting from the shackles of self-restraint and springing forward to kiss her on the cheek. He had been unable control himself. She was afraid to name the unbridled passion she knew was buried within his chest. She sighed contentedly, touched the spot on her cheek where he had kissed her, then carefully transplanted the touch to puckered lips.

She jumped out of bed. From her bureau she grabbed a jean skirt and a pink pullover top. While she was dressing, she looked at her sleeping sister. Matilda had been reprimanded the night before, after she and Archibald were late returning to the house. It was funny, thought Holly, that Matilda had used the lame, improbable excuse of being lost in the woods behind the pond. It was an obvious fib, but Holly had said nothing. She was too absorbed in her own concerns to get involved in her sister's shenanigans. Well, at least Matilda had the advantage of being a girl, and had avoided the spanking that her dad had applied to Archibald's rear.

Holly tied the laces on her riding boots and slipped quietly from the bedroom. She tiptoed down the hall, sprang lightly down the steps, skipped through the foyer, and rushed out the front door. It was a bright, crisp morning. She wanted to take Dan on a warm-up ride to Aylor's Store, then return to the house in time to have breakfast with Emmet and Warren.

Henry was standing by his tractor when Holly ran into barn. He held a container of flux in one hand and a coil of solder in the other. Beside him on the ground was a butane torch. He was preparing to patch a leaky radiator.

"Morning, Dad," Holly chirped.

"Good morning, Holly. Up and at 'em mighty early, aren't ya? I guess you're getting pretty excited about Saturday."

"Am I ever!" Holly beamed.

"You'll do just fine. I have a whole lot of faith in you."

"Thanks. Hey, Dad, are you sure it's safe for you to use that torch in here?"

Henry glanced at the dry hay behind him. "No, I reckon not. I believe I'll pull the tractor outside."

"Good thinking, Dad. See ya later." Holly skipped toward the back of the barn. Dan neighed excitedly when he saw her coming. He stretched his neck over the stall door and with practiced lips unhooked the wooden latch. Holly shook her head as he pranced forward and nudged her with his nose. "Look at you, Dan," she teased. "You're more excited about Saturday than I am."

Emmet and Warren awoke early, had breakfast, and were out of the house before Holly returned. They fetched Senator from the fort and by eight A.M. were standing by the side of Route 631 with their thumbs poised. The idea was to hitchhike to Binkerton for the day and be home in time for supper. As Emmet explained, the purpose of their trip was to inspect the parade route and choose the best location for viewing events on Saturday.

Although it mattered not a whit to Warren or Senator, Emmet's real purpose was to see if Mike Cunningham was setting up a booth in the pavilion, and if so, to see if his daughter was assisting him in that endeavor.

Clementine remained in bed until after nine. She had hardly slept during the night. Now she was beset with morning sickness. The baby in her womb was making nutritive demands on her system, and the drain left her feeling nauseous and weak. Yet this physical discomfort did not detract from her spiritual and emotional contentment.

She swirled her fingertips softly over the swelling in her belly and whispered, "Hello, little one."

Archibald spent the morning lurking in the hedge by the garden. He had agreed to return the carpet to its hiding place under the bed and now was watching for his mother to step outside so he could sneak in unobserved. Eventually she did appear in the yard, where she yawned and stretched her limbs, then meandered up to the apple orchard on the ridge. It was the opportunity Archibald was waiting for. He grabbed the carpet from the bushes and scurried toward the house.

Matilda spent most of Monday alone in her special sitting spot in the woods. She wished to savor Sunday's achievement in solitude. Also she wanted to construct a mental chronology of events before the details got fuzzy. Already the physical sensation of flying had begun to fade, and the quality of her memories was beginning to take on the character of dream fragments. Half in jest, she pinched her leg above the knee. The bruise that appeared on her thigh confirmed she was awake.

It really did happen, she told herself. Extraordinary. We achieved textile aviation. I deserve to be congratulated. After all, I collected the clues. It was my persistence that led to the successful flight. And not only did we fly and land safely, we did it without getting caught. Only Archibald and I know the secret, and he will keep his trap shut. I must admit it was pretty smart for me to remind him that he was the culprit who trespassed in Mom and Dad's room and stole the rug. Good going, Matilda.

It is doubtful Matilda would have felt so smug if she'd known that on Sunday evening, under the cover of dusk, three shadowy figures had been hiding in some trees on a farm near Binkerton. They were there with the intention of stealing the farmer's geese after dark. It was totally by chance that one of them happened to turn his head and see a flying object. He looked at it long enough to ascertain that it was not a mirage, then alerted his uncle.

Crowley Hogget nearly fell out of his tree when he looked and saw the passing marvel.

Emmet was pretty disappointed when he and his companions arrived in Binkerton and learned that Mike Cunningham would not arrive at the pavilion until Wednesday. As far as he was concerned, the trip was a wash. It was merely for the sake of appearances that he took time to show Warren around town.

Yet it was soon obvious to Warren that Emmet did not want to be there. He frowned a lot, and took almost no interest in the parade route. Consequently Warren was more curious than surprised when Emmet informed him it was time to go. "Why?" Warren asked. "Seems like we just got here."

"I'm just ready to go."

"Don't you want to get a milk shake first, or something?"

"Listen, Warren . . . we're really not supposed to be here without permission. We would get restricted if Dad knew."

"What's the matter? You can tell me," Warren said.

Emmet glanced up and down the street, adjusted his belt, then looked in Warren's eyes. "You like Holly, don't you?"

"She's all right," Warren mumbled.

"All right? You kissed her on the cheek the other night. That must mean you think she's more than just all right."

Warren's jaw twitched as he bowed his head and blushed. "What was I supposed to do? She said it was an honored custom in the South for visitors to kiss the oldest daughter of the host."

"You fell for that?"

"Yes, I fell for it. So what? As a matter of fact, it sounded like a pretty good custom to me. You don't mind, do you?"

Emmet smiled. "Oh, it's only natural, I suppose. I don't mind, really. But I still want to head back home. I'd hate to be restricted and miss the festival. You see . . . well, there's somebody I wouldn't mind observing a custom with myself."

"Contessa?"

Emmet nodded.

"In that case, let's get going."

"You're backing up if you're waiting for me," said Emmet.

The trio marched to the shaded intersection of Lacy Lane and Caroline Street and positioned themselves for hitchhiking. The traffic was all but nonexistent; perhaps one car in ten minutes. Some folks slowed to get a good look at Senator—a few offered wisecracks through open windows—but none offered a ride. Next they moved to the shadeless intersection at Hopewell Street. Their luck here was the same, except now they fried in the sun. Eventually Emmet declared, "I say we hoof it. Better than dying here in a standstill."

It was a three-mile walk from Hopewell to Route 631, then thirteen more miles back to Aylor's Store. After walking less than one mile, Senator began to complain and lag behind the boys. Warren felt sorry for the little monkey. He whistled and invited Senator to ride on his back. Senator wasted no time in accepting the offer. Once ensconced upon Warren's strong shoulders, he appreciatively patted the boy's wavy hair.

By the time they arrived at Route 631, both boys were sweating profusely. Emmet pointed to a shady spot at the side of the road where they could rest. As soon as they plopped down in the shade, a dilapidated Jeep approached from the east. Neither boy bothered to stand and hoist a thumb. Ironically, it was the first vehicle to stop after it went by them. It shifted into reverse and backed up until it was even with the trio. Emmet jumped to his feet and looked at the three men in the vehicle, waiting to see if they intended to offer a ride. The men just looked at him for a few seconds, then turned to confer among themselves. Then, without bothering to wave or say a word, the engine revved and the Jeep lurched forward.

The man driving was none other than Crowley Hogget.

"Wonder what those guys wanted," said Warren.

"They didn't look civilized to me."

"I wouldn't have ridden anywhere with them."

"Me either, although I am mighty tired of walking."

"Me too. Walking puts a monkey on my back."

"You freeloader," Emmet laughed, pointing at Senator. "You're smarter than the both of us put together."

Senator squealed and flipped backward. He landed on his hands, wiggled his legs, rotated his hips, swung sideways, and spiraled back to his feet. Then he took a deep bow.

"He's humble, too," Warren said.

"Yeah. Senator has style," Emmet said proudly, then quickly turned toward the road. A silver pickup truck was traveling in their direction. "Here we go." Emmet cocked his thumb.

"Come on. Be nice," prayed Warren.

146

"Pleeease," Emmet intoned.

The pickup slowed and pulled to the side. The boys rushed forward to meet the driver. He seemed friendly. Emmet had a vague notion that he'd seen him before. The driver leaned toward the passenger window and called, "How far you fellows heading?"

"A dozen miles . . . to 628," Emmet answered.

"I can drop you at the fork above Aylor's Store."

"Perfect. Thanks."

"I've got room up front for one of you and the monkey. One of you has to get in the back."

"Go ahead, Warren. I'll take the back. You carried him most of the way." Emmet darted to the rear of the truck, which was covered with a camper hull. He hopped through the opening over the tailgate and began to crawl toward the cab window to signal that he was safely inside. But someone else tapped at the window before he could reach it. It took a second for his eyes to adjust in the dim light, and when they did, he could hardly believe what they were seeing. There was Contessa Cunningham, sitting in the corner smiling in his direction.

Emmet rocked back on his heels.

Contessa giggled and looked shyly at her feet.

"Is that your father? I didn't recognize him."

"Yes," Contessa replied.

"Where's his monkey? I've got one too, you know."

"She's at home. I saw yours get up front."

Emmet found a place to sit, then struggled to think of what to say. Contessa waited in silence. Eventually an idea occurred to him. "How do you do?"

"Fine." Contessa brushed a wisp of brown hair from her face. Emmet thought it looked like the face of an earthbound angel with brown eyes. "And you?" she asked politely.

"Oh, I'm fine too," Emmet answered just as the truck hit a bump in the road. He bounced up and banged his head against the

147

camper hull, then landed back where he had been sitting. Contessa could hardly suppress her laugh.

"Do you remember me?" Emmet blurted.

"Of course I do." Contessa smiled. "You're Emmet."

"That's right. I'm Emmet." He grinned. "And you're Contessa. It sure is nice to see you again. A real pleasure. I was thinking about you just the other day."

"You were thinking about me?"

"Yes, I was. And also, a couple of weeks ago, I named a boat after you. It helped save my life before it fell apart."

"Excuse me?" Contessa leaned forward.

"Actually it was a raft. Warren—that's him in the front—he's a buddy of mine from New Hampshire—his parents are dead—he and I and Senator—that's my monkey's name—we got caught in Weeping Willow Swamp during the flood. We had to make a raft to escape."

"I heard. You had the whole county out looking for you."

"That was us," Emmet boasted. "We got pretty messed up in there. I wasn't scared, though."

"And the raft that saved you . . . you named it after me?"

"Yes."

The truck shifted into a lower gear, reduced speed, and pulled onto the shoulder of the road. Before Emmet could pose the question himself, Contessa asked, "Are you going to be at the Binkerton Festival?"

"Darn tootin' I am. My sister Holly is riding point. Are you going to be there?"

"Yes. I'm working with Dad in his booth," Contessa said as the vehicle came to a stop. "You'd be welcome if you wanted to come by and visit."

"I'll be there." Emmet prepared to jump. "Now that you've invited me, it'd take a hurricane to keep me away."

"Good-bye," called Contessa.

"So long," said Emmet, his spirits soaring as his body sailed over the tailgate. Unfortunately he banged his head against a strip of metal trim on the camper hull, lost his balance, and tumbled into the road. Ignoring the jolt of pain, he jumped up and waved. As Mike Cunningham let out the clutch, a puff of exhaust smoke issued from the tailpipe and enveloped him in a blue cloud. He stumbled woozily toward the ditch and sneezed.

"What happened to you?" Warren rushed to Emmet's side.

"What do you mean?"

"What do I mean? You've got blood running down from behind your ear, there are tears in your eyes, and you're wobbling like a drunk. That's what I mean," declared Warren.

"I saw Contessa," Emmet pointed. "She was in the back."

"She did that to you?"

"No. I did. It was an accident." Emmet sat down and put a hand to the side of his head. A rivulet of blood trickled over his fingers. "That was the best ride I've ever had."

Warren looked doubtfully at his pal. "You know, Emmet, you Southerners are mighty hard to figure sometimes."

In a word, complicated describes the meeting that Emma Bean attended on Monday. The stated purpose of the gathering in the White House basement was for Emma to give a status report on her training program. But no one besides Graves Copeland cared an iota about her classes. It was the Zandinski Box that interested the other officials. Of this, Emma was reluctant to share her assessment. She knew the group would not like what she had to report. But rather than drop that bomb up front, she opened the floor to questions.

"Tell me something, miss," commanded General Batter. "If you were to aim this contraption at a military strategist, would you be able to discern what he was thinking?"

Major Sue Wright coughed into her gloved hand.

The General glanced at her before amending his question. "Would you be able to discern what he, or she, was thinking?"

"Maybe," said Emma.

"What do you mean, maybe?" snapped Bob Thrax. He did not intend to be rude; it was just that he was high-strung.

"I mean that maybe I would be able to discern what said military strategist was thinking," Emma said dryly. "Or maybe not."

"What *would* you know if you aimed the Box at a strategist? Military or otherwise," asked Graves Copeland.

"It depends on the circumstances. I might not know a thing."

"The Zandinski Box is effective in correlating asynchronous events, not in reading minds," interjected Simmons. From the look the others in the room gave him, or did not give him, it was apparent his input garnered small respect.

"Might not know a thing," muttered General Batter. "Please inform us, miss: In what manner should the Box be employed?"

"None whatsoever." Emma could no longer evade the truth.

Jaws dropped, legs crossed, and eyeballs rolled.

"Why not?" asked Janet Libson. She was at the meeting to take notes, not speak, but no one seemed to mind the breach in protocol. It was the question on everyone's lips.

"The Box is a placebo," said Emma. "It does not work."

"Now just wait a second." General Batter jumped up and shook a finger at Emma. "The Box has been tested numerous times. It has been proven to work. Don't give us this crap about a placebo."

Major Wright coughed into her hand again. General Batter quit shaking his finger and sat down.

"Miss Bean," said Graves Copeland in a smooth, diplomatic tone, "would you kindly elaborate? The General is correct. The Zandinski Box has tested positively in the past."

Emma liked Graves. He seemed reasonable. "Yes, I know. But all of the tests were made with proven psychics operating the Box. I participated in many of them myself. It is my belief that similar

150

results would have been, or could be, obtained with just about any instrument."

"Any instrument?" Bob Thrax was aghast.

"Well, perhaps not a banana, or a toaster. A person must believe in the placebo before it will work."

There was an audible gasp in the room. Then Simmons, Bob Thrax, and General Batter began to squabble.

fifteen

THEY NABBED ARCHIBALD at four in the afternoon. He had been to visit Carl at the store and was on his way home when they crept up on him from behind. All he saw was a gloved hand. It reached into view and forced a cloth gag into his mouth. The next thing he knew he was engulfed by a burlap sack. Then he was hoisted onto a man's shoulder, carried a short distance, and dumped onto the floorboard of an idling vehicle. A door slammed shut. The vehicle drove away. No one in the store heard the muffler backfire. He had been kidnapped without a clue.

One of the captors used a booted foot to apply pressure to the small of Archibald's back. All fifty-five pounds of young Dither were spread as flatly upon the floorboard as the sack would permit. A snarl of rope and a discarded liquor bottle jabbed painfully against his stomach. The stench of manure mixed with kerosene permeated his nostrils. He wanted to faint, yet he kept his senses and tried to determine what was happening. He guessed from the sounds around him that the vehicle was an old farm truck. It needed shock absorbers. He was jostled at every bump in the road. The booted foot rode his back like a pedal. Through the shabbily patched floorboard he could hear the pinging of a hot engine, the whining of a tired transmission, and the popping of an exhausted muffler.

He was scared. In the seven years of his life he had known many *instances* of fear—flashes that came and went in nanoseconds of physical reaction, or confused interludes of projected mental trouble—but this was his first experience with a fear that fed on itself and would not cease when he told it to go away. The fright he experienced during the carpet flight was reassuring compared to the terror he now felt. His previously unchallenged assumption that he would live forever was suddenly called into question. He remembered bragging to Carl at the store one day: "I don't give a fat bullfrog about nothing unless it sallies up and smacks me in the face. Even then I'd rather run than worry about it." Now he could not run. He wondered if he was meeting his fate. It was all too evident that his incarceration in the burlap sack was not intended as a joke. He felt a cold seriousness in the stamp of the booted foot riding his back to the floorboard.

After what Archibald guessed was twenty minutes (it may have been ten), the truck slowed and turned off the paved road. It proceeded in low gear, rising and dropping over erratic bumps and sometimes pitching unevenly to one side. Archibald figured they were traveling on an old logging road or on a fire trail through the woods. His supposition was confirmed when he heard branches smack at the hood and windshield. From within his smelly sack, he invoked prayers for the vehicle to topple and provide him with a chance to escape. It never happened. The bottom-heavy Jeep continued to plow forward.

Archibald was beginning to wonder if he was going to go numb and die in the sack when he heard the screech of worn brake shoes grinding against iron drums. The vehicle lurched to a halt. The engine was silenced. Two doors creaked open, and the pressure from the booted foot was removed from his back. He was promptly jerked from the floorboard and hoisted onto a square shoulder. He was carried upside down with his head dangling backward, slapping against his captor's back. Compared to the floorboard, this seemed a relatively comfortable position. At least now there was room in the sack for him to wiggle and let blood circulate. As he began to squirm and stretch, he heard, for the first time since his abduction, the gravelly voice of one of his abductors. It was a cruel, commanding voice. "Hold tight to that weasel," it carped. "Don't let him get away between here and the hideout."

After being toted a hundred yards through what felt like a briar patch, Archibald heard a door creak open. By now he had determined there were three captors. This was confirmed by the sound of six feet clopping on the floor of the room they entered. The door slammed. Archibald was tossed in a corner. By dint of luck he landed on his rear end. It took several seconds for his head to clear. As soon as he could see straight, he began to peek through the loose weave of the burlap sack. Three shapes, one much larger than the others. The big shape coughed phlegm from his throat and rasped, "I've got something I gotta do. I'm taking the Jeep. You idiots will eat rocks if that runt finds a way to escape."

"Got it, Crowley."

"I told you not to use my name!"

"Oops. Sorry, boss."

"You stupid nincompoops!" Crowley stormed from the room.

Archibald trembled and wondered what would happen next.

At ten after six that evening, ninety minutes after Crowley had left the hideout and twenty minutes before suppertime on Dither Farm, Clementine hung her apron on its hook and went looking for Holly. She found her daughter in the parlor. With a rapid motion of an index finger, she signaled for her to follow. "It's your night to set the table. Come along now. I have something I would like to discuss with you."

Holly formed a question mark with her face and climbed reluctantly from her chair. "Am I in trouble?"

"No, sweetheart. I just want to speak with you."

"You mean talk, like back and forth?"

"Yes, Holly."

"Whew." Holly trailed her mother into the kitchen and went straight to the cupboard, where she began withdrawing plates. As she placed them around the table, she asked, "So, Mom, what's up?"

Clementine sat on a stool. She looked serious, Holly thought, but not angry. She smoothed her dress over her swelling belly and sighed. "First I wanted to say that Henry and I are very happy that you've been selected to lead the Binkerton parade. It's a mighty good reflection on all us Dithers."

"On Dan, too," Holly added.

"Yes, him too. You must feel very proud."

"Mom, I'm so proud I'm about to burst."

Clementine paused a moment. "Holly . . ." She waited until she had her daughter's complete attention. "Pride is a good thing to have in yourself, but you should consider that most people are offended when they see outward displays of it. Too much pride is, well . . . it's not a good thing."

"What do you mean?" Holly was on the defensive. "Are you trying to tell me I'm a show-off? Is that it?"

"I did not say that," Clementine replied softly. "I was speaking of personal pride, and how best to express it."

"I don't get it. You and Dad are always telling us that we should be proud of ourselves."

"As you should, Holly, on the inside. I am not criticizing your confidence, sweetheart. I merely wish to share with you—as a gift from mother to daughter—the knowledge that modesty never fails

155

to make a favorable impression on people. Or at least not on good people. Also, I should add, modesty is an especially attractive trait when it is seen in someone as talented as you."

Holly felt a surge of shame. She looked down for a second, then dashed into Clementine's open arms. In a gush of emotion she confessed, "You're right, Mom. I'm a glory hog. I admit it. My ego is completely out of control. I'm always thinking of ways to get attention." Holly rested her head upon her mother's swollen belly and sobbed. "I just can't stop thinking of me."

"Don't cry, Holly. You're not a glory hog. What you are is an exuberant, irresistible ball of fire." Clementine ran her fingers through Holly's curly hair. "All of us Dithers have large doses of personality. I would never try to take that away. All I'm suggesting is for you to keep a little modesty in mind when you sit in the spotlight this coming Saturday. That's all. Okay?"

Holly sniffled. "I'll try."

Clementine kissed the crown of her daughter's head. "Bless you. You're going to go to the top one day."

Holly wiped the tears from her cheeks and grinned at her mother. "I've always thought so too. Only now I'm not going to advertise it so much."

"That's the spirit," Clementine laughed, and turned her daughter toward the door. "Now go gather everyone for supper."

Holly ran to the front foyer, stood at the bottom of the steps facing the screen door to the porch, and lifted her soprano voice to its full capacity: *"Time for supper!"*

Henry was the last person to enter the kitchen. He glanced at Archibald's empty chair as he pulled his own from the table and sat down. "Is he tardy again?"

"Two nights in one week," Clementine affirmed.

"Where is he?" Henry asked the family.

"Haven't seen him." Emmet shrugged.

"He was here for lunch," Holly noted.

"I think he went to play marbles with Carl," said Emmet.

"He's not there. I just came from the store," said Henry.

"Matilda, what do you know about this?" Clementine turned to her youngest daughter.

"Nothing," Matilda lied. She did not know what else to do. An hour earlier, when she had gone to check the mailbox at the end of the driveway, a giant redneck man had been hiding in the weeds by the gate. After nearly scaring her to death, he had informed her that Archibald was in his custody and would not be released until she presented him with the flying carpet. "I know you got one. So don't argue," the man had said. He then threatened to slit Archibald's throat if she blabbed to her parents or the police. He told her to meet him with the carpet by the gate, at midnight tonight. When she did, he told her, he would give her her brother in exchange for the rug.

"Are you sure? You look like you know something."

"No, Mom, I don't." It hurt Matilda to lie. She tried her best to sound normal.

"We'll start without him." Henry rolled up his sleeves and grabbed a fork. "Archibald will get his due when he gets home."

Back at the hideout, Acorn and Bart were growing impatient. Archibald had them on edge. After having been silent for two hours, he had suddenly begun to chant, "I can't take it anymore. I gotta go pee. I can't take it anymore. I gotta go pee." This went on for about five minutes.

Finally Acorn could not take it anymore. The agony in the voice coming from the sack touched a soft spot in his heart. (Acorn was the older, more intelligent of the two nephews.) He cupped his hands over his ears and told his brother Bart, "The kid is driving me bonkers."

"Reckon we ought to let him out?" asked Bart. Bart was an

inveterate question asker. It was the only way he related.

"When ya gotta go, ya gotta go," Acorn said sympathetically. He and his brother were not really bad people. They had been led into the crime by Crowley and only continued because of the threat of violence he held over them. "He can pee out the back window. I'll watch him. You keep an eye peeled for Crowley."

"You mean the boss?"

"Yes, the boss," Acorn snapped. Then in a milder tone he said to Archibald, "Okay, kid. Quit complaining. I'm gonna let you go. But afterward ya gotta get back in the sack."

Archibald did not move or look at his captors as the sack was removed. He stood with arms flat at his sides and his chin on his chest, in the style of prisoners in war movies he had seen on television. He followed without resistance when Acorn took him by the wrist and led him to a broken window, the only window, in the rear of the one-room shack. Acorn turned his back so that Archibald had some privacy. The boy quickly took aim and went about his business, finishing with a heartfelt sigh of relief. Then he bowed his head and trudged obediently back to his corner. A scorned puppy could not have looked more pathetic.

"Don't pout, kid," Acorn jested. "We ain't gonna kill you tonight."

Archibald was allowed to remain out of his sack for a few minutes so he could eat. Bart handed him a sardine-and-cracker sandwich, which he hungrily devoured. The food reminded him of what he was missing.

Sad but true: At the very moment Archibald was licking the dry crumbs from his lips, his mother was standing in her clean kitchen, slicing into one of the many fruit pies she had baked in preparation for the Pie and Pastry Division of the BIF Culinary Competition. As the knife glided through the delicate crust, the air around her filled with a cherry aroma. It cast a sensory spell over everyone in the kitchen. For more than the next five minutes, young Archibald was a forgotten boy.

After his second helping of pie, Henry pushed back from the table. "Award winning," he said to Clementine. Then he pointed to Emmet. "Come on, son. It's *your* turn to help me look for Archibald this time. Warren, you come with us. We'll check the store again, and if he isn't there we'll go by Leopold's."

It was Matilda's night to wash the dishes. She could not concentrate. By the time she placed the last dry plate in its proper cabinet, she had developed a bad case of nervous jitters. She had to get outside, where she could think. In keeping with house rules, she reported to Clementine that the chore was complete, then excused herself from the parlor.

She left the house and went to sit by the creek. The moon was early in its first quarter. She wished she were sitting on it instead of on earth, where everything around her spelled trouble. Events had gotten entirely out of hand. Time was acting quirky, and Crowley had left her with a one-sided coin to toss. There were no options. She could not risk doing anything that might lead to Archibald's having his throat slit. "He has me," Matilda told the moon. "I have to give the rug to the ugly man."

Leopold, who had not been himself of late, had been staring for a long time at a bowl of stewed tomatoes when he heard Henry's truck arrive in the yard. He pushed aside his meal and went to the dining-room window. Somehow he knew as soon as he saw Henry's face that one of the kids was in trouble. How he knew, he could not say. But when he stepped outside and learned that Henry was indeed looking for Archibald, an alarm went off in his elongated, white-haired noggin. The doting Leopold snapped out of a week-long funk and began transforming himself from daydreaming bachelor into ace detective. His longing for Emma Bean suddenly vanished. He had begun to apply himself to the case at hand. Call it a hunch, say a bullfrog told him, whatever; Leopold sensed immediately that Archibald had met with foul play. He looked at Henry, Emmet, and Warren. They stared back with blank faces. Leopold had another hunch. "Have you checked with Matilda? Does she know anything?"

"Says she doesn't," Henry answered. "Neither do Holly, Clementine, and the boys. It's strange. Carl remembers Archibald leaving for home right at four o'clock. I can't figure how anyone could get lost between the store and the farm."

Leopold considered for a moment, then laid a hand on Henry's shoulder. "Let's drive over to Flea's place and see if Archibald is there. If he isn't . . . you might want to rally up another search party."

"A search party?" Henry huffed. "What kind of suggestion is that? Where do you think he is?"

"I suggest nothing, yet," Leopold answered. "Let's speak to Flea first. No use rushing to any conclusions."

"That's like shooting a dead skunk," interjected Emmet.

"Correct," said Leopold. "We must approach this logically."

"Approach it however you want, Leopold." Henry moved toward the truck. "I just want to find Arch and go home."

After Crowley left Matilda, he got his Jeep from the woods beyond the driveway and drove to the Hot Spot in Binkerton. He deserved a few whiskeys. How better to reflect on the new life he would soon be leading. As far as Crowley could figure, there was no limit on the size of the fortune he would soon fetch for the flying carpet. He figured he would start the bidding at a million dollars. If Hollywood didn't scarf it up at that price, he felt certain the Pentagon would. Maybe a million isn't enough, he chuckled to himself. Maybe I ought to make it two million.

After a couple hours of drinking, Crowley paid his tab and left the Hot Spot. He slouched in the driver's seat of the battered Jeep and drove cautiously through town. He did not want to attract Sheriff Ludwell's attention. The hideout, which had been the office for a now-defunct sawmill, was perfectly hidden in a forest of scrub pine. It must remain a secret.

He parked the Jeep in a thicket fifty yards from the hut and crept quietly forward. He wanted to surprise his nephews to see if he could catch them napping. He tiptoed to the door, then kicked it open and charged into the room. Acorn and Bart were playing cards, but they had Archibald in plain view in front of them.

"You done a good job," Crowley grunted. The nephews relaxed. (Sometimes when Crowley had been drinking, he was almost a decent person.) But Archibald did not relax. Shivers ran up his spine as Crowley turned his attention upon him. The sack had been tied around his neck like a collar so that his head was exposed. It was the first time Crowley and Archibald had seen each other face-to-face. For the young captive it was an exceptionally unpleasant experience. Crowley moved toward him and pretended he was going to kick the sack. Archibald instinctively turned to avoid the blow. His reaction caused Crowley to laugh. Crowley loved it when people were afraid of him. He bent over and grabbed Archibald by an ear. The smell of liquor was pervasive. Archibald quivered, afraid of what might happen. Crowley exposed his yellowing teeth in a maniacal grin and said to Acorn and Bart, "Look at this little weasel. He sure is ugly for his size. I don't think either of you boys was that ugly until you were twice his age. I do hope his sister decides to cooperate. Looking at him now, it worries me she might not want him back."

Archibald suppressed the urge to tell Crowley to look in a mirror if he wanted to see ugly. Instead he lowered his eyes. He knew who he was dealing with. Crowley was one of the men who had ganged up on his father. He wished his dad was there now. He needed help. No seven-year-old in the world was a match against three grown men. A tear formed in his eye, skidded down his cheek, then landed on his lips. The taste of salt gave him sudden courage. He glared defiantly at Crowley and visualized conking him on his fat head with a frying pan.

The reader has probably noticed how this story, which began at a slow crawl through a tranquil, rural environment, has picked up speed and now seems to be racing forward. A mere thirty days have passed since Great-Aunt Emma Bean appeared at the Dithers' front gate, and yet during this period more abnormal events have occurred in Willow County than usually occur in two, maybe three years. Certainly by now (whether the reader has noticed or not) each member of the Dither family was conscious of the accelerating rate of unusual events.

On this particular night, as the clock passed nine, with but four and a half days remaining before the Binkerton Independence Festival parade, there was no one in Willow County more concerned about the increasing event-to-time ratio than Matilda. She in fact was terrified. Time had become for her a rope burn. She felt a desperate need for assistance in fighting the deadline. And *dead*line was what it would be, she reminded herself, if she failed to meet the challenge. She was hesitant about sharing her secret with her sister. Holly could help distract Clementine so the carpet could be retrieved from the bedroom, and she might provide physical and moral support later, when it was time to rendezvous with the kidnapper. But what could Matilda tell her? Would Holly believe the actual truth? And if she did, would she get excited and spill the beans? That would spell disaster for Archibald.

In the final analysis, Matilda decided she had to enlist someone's help. Since Emmet and Warren were with Henry, Holly had to be trusted.

It was nine thirty when Matilda found her sister in their bedroom. "Holly, will you do a huge favor for me?" she asked. "Probably the biggest favor I'll ever ask in my whole life?"

"What is it?" Holly asked casually. She had not caught the seriousness in Matilda's voice.

"It's about Archibald. But before I ask you, you have to swear not to say a word to anyone."

"I swear. What do you know about Archibald?" Holly suddenly was interested.

"Swear again. You didn't sound like you meant it."

Holly put her right hand over her heart. "I swear. I won't tell a soul whatever it is you tell me. There, I said it. Now, what about Archibald?"

"His life is in danger."

"How? What are you talking about?"

"He's been kidnapped."

"Are you kidding?"

"No. I'm absolutely serious. I wouldn't kid about a thing like that."

"How do you know?"

"Holly . . . if there was more time, I'd explain. I promise I'll tell you everything later. But right now I need your help—Archibald needs your help. What I want you to do is distract Mom from the house. I have to do something without her seeing me."

"I just had a good talk with Mom. I don't think I want to play any tricks on her."

"Please, Holly," Matilda pleaded. "It's a matter of life and death. Please. If you don't help, Archibald might die. And if he died, well, everyone would be so upset that I'm sure the parade would be canceled."

Holly thought for a second. "All right, Matilda, I'll help you. For Archibald's sake. Now, what do you want me to do?"

"Go in the barn and start screaming. When Mom gets there,

pretend like you saw a snake or something. I only need about two minutes alone in the house. If she asks what you were doing in the barn, say you were looking for Archibald. Will you do it?"

"Just remember, you promised to explain everything."

"I will."

Unfortunately, the girls' ploy was foiled before Holly ever left the bedroom. While she and Matilda were talking, fourteen men in five separate vehicles had driven down the driveway. Suddenly the yard was full of people. Matilda leaned from the window and listened. Her heart sank when she heard that Sheriff Ludwell had been called and was on his way to the farm in a squad car. "Oh, no," she lamented. "The kidnapper will think I ratted on him."

"Do you still want me to go scream in the barn?"

"Too late." Matilda was on the verge of tears.

Holly moved to comfort her sister with a hug. "Better give me the scoop, Matilda. Maybe I can think of something."

Clementine swooned and had to steady herself against the back of a chair when Henry confessed that he agreed with Leopold, who believed Archibald had somehow met with foul play. She fell to the floor after Henry explained, "Ten of us beat the bushes for two hours. We looked in every well within walking distance. Wade Butcher's dogs couldn't pick up a scent. If he was around here, we would have found him."

Leopold was standing with Henry when Clementine dropped. He bent over and checked her pulse, then pushed open an eyelid and peered into a green iris. "She's fainted," Leopold proclaimed. "She'll be all right. Give me a hand here, Henry. Let's put her upstairs in bed. Flea and Bellamonte should be here soon to look after her. Let's you and I get going and find Archibald."

sixteen

SHERIFF NEWTON LUDWELL arrived at Dither Farm while Henry and Leopold were upstairs putting Clementine to bed. Emmet, Warren, Senator, and a dozen men were scattered about in the front yard when the officer drove up in his unmarked Plymouth Fury. The men had gathered there to wait for Henry and Leopold to tell them what to do. Some stood with hands in pockets, some with arms crossed, others sipped at cups of coffee drawn from a thermos on the tailgate of Garland Barlow's pickup. They were a quiet, stern group. Not one of them said a word as the sheriff stopped in the driveway and stepped out of his squad car.

The Aylor's Store crowd was not overly fond of Newton Ludwell. Their dislike was not based on the fact that Newton was from Binkerton—that was forgivable. The men did not like him because he was a man big on theories and short on general substance. Also, he was arrogant. There had not been a capital crime perpetrated in Willow County for more than twenty years, but Newton comported himself with the swank confidence of a big-city cop. Jimmy Aylor pretty much summed up their collective opinion when he remarked, "I've known Newton Ludwell for years, and I doubt seriously if he could outwit a brick."

The Willowites, though not enamored of the person, were civil toward the law. They watched silently as Newton adjusted the holster on his hips and swaggered toward the center of their group. He paused before he spoke, rubbing his chin and surveying the collection of men as if checking them against profiles on wanted posters. "What's this I hear about a boy missing?"

"That's right," Garland nodded.

Newton waited. There was an extended silence. "This one of the same boys who was lost in the swamp during the flood?"

"Nope," Jimmy answered.

"Different boy?"

"Yep."

"How long has this one been missing?"

"Awhile," said Wade Butcher.

"Just how long is awhile?" Newton sounded angry.

"Since earlier this afternoon."

"Any ideas where he might have gotten to?"

"Nope."

"Where's Henry?"

"Inside." Felton Fibbs motioned with a thumb.

"You sure are a helpful lot," Newton remarked sourly.

"Well, thank you," said Jimmy.

"No, thank *you* for cooperating with my investigation," huffed Sheriff Ludwell as he started toward the house.

"Happy to oblige," added John Washington.

Holly and Matilda huddled in the hallway outside the door to their parents' bedroom, waiting for Leopold and Henry to exit. Matilda had done her best to explain the situation to Holly. Now she was on the verge of a breakdown. She bit her lower lip and stared woefully at the floor. "It isn't all your fault," Holly said to console her sister.

Matilda knew differently. "Yes it is. As soon as this nightmare is over, I'm going to commit suicide."

"That's the coward's way out," puffed Holly. "Wait until we know for sure that Mom is all right, then I'll help you decide what to do about that stupid kidnapper."

"But we need the rug. There's no way we can get to it now." Matilda's face fell. Her world had been turned inside out. Even she and her sister had switched roles: Holly was innocent and was being helpful, while she was guilty and feeling helpless. "It's no use," she moaned.

"Matilda, we have to try."

"Try what?"

"We'll think of something. Trust me." Holly perked with conviction. "I'm not having the parade canceled because of some dumb bully." Her words were punctuated by a knock at the back door. She ran down to see who it was. Sheriff Ludwell had poked his head into the hallway. "May I help you?" Holly asked. The fearful notion that the policeman had come for Matilda skipped quickly through Holly's mind.

"Where's your father?" asked Sheriff Ludwell.

"With Mom," Holly sighed. "She fainted. Come on, I'll show you." Holly started up the stairs, but stopped short when she came face-to-kneecap with Leopold, who was coming down. He peered over her head and greeted the uniformed officer. "Newton."

"Mr. Hillacre," replied the sheriff.

"Please wait in the parlor." Leopold gestured vaguely. "Mrs. Dither fainted. Henry and I will join you in a minute."

"Okay, but I haven't got all night."

No sooner did Newton select a chair and make himself comfortable than Flea Jenfries entered the house without knocking and breezed past the parlor entrance. When Newton saw her go by, he

167

rose partially from his chair. Flea barely acknowledged him with a nod before darting up the stairs. When she arrived on the upper floor, she found Henry sitting in the hallway with his arms placed protectively around Matilda and Holly. They looked like a trio of frightened refugees. Flea flapped forward and pecked them each on the head with a kiss. "Goodness gracious," she swore. "What's this summer coming to?"

"Wish I knew," said Henry. "Clementine is in there."

"Henry, don't worry about her. She'll bounce back. You've got Archibald to think of now."

Just then Leopold stepped into the hallway. "Flea, I'm mighty glad you're here."

"How is she?"

"Distressed, but otherwise fine. Just keep her calm."

"Of course. And you . . ." Flea gave Leopold a quick hug and whispered in his ear, "You're the smartest man in Willow County. I expect you to find Archibald."

"I will," Leopold avowed. Then he tapped Henry on the shoulder. "Come on. Let's go speak with the sheriff."

Meanwhile the men in the yard were growing restless. They were uncertain whether to continue waiting or to resume the hunt on their own. Everyone agreed they only wanted to do what was best. Jimmy Aylor announced with emotion, "I'd go to hell and back for any one of Henry's kids."

"Hear, hear," voiced several others.

The sentiment rang strong. Both Felton Fibbs and John Washington swore off the bottle until little Archibald was back in his mother's arms.

Warren and Emmet had been standing a few feet away from the men, unseen in the background. As Emmet listened to the proclamations of loyalty and respect toward his father, a lump grew in his throat and he thought he might cry. Silently he climbed over the fence and wandered out into the adjoining field. Unbeknownst to him, a concerned Senator followed at a respectful distance.

And so, at ten thirty on that fated Monday night, everyone concerned with Archibald's whereabouts was present on Dither Farm. Everyone except for Carl Plummers. Like a mountain of great sorrow, he sat alone in the dark store and stared into the long summer night. In one of his chubby hands he held Archibald's favorite taw, and with all the might he could muster, he concentrated on the safe return of his friend and partner.

After Flea observed Clementine for a few moments, she determined that her distraught friend would benefit immensely from the restorative gift of sleep. She dipped into her proverbial bag of tricks and withdrew a vial and an eyedropper. The vial contained extract of valerian root, Flea's remedy for insomnia. She put ten drops of the sedative in a glass of water and instructed Clementine to drink.

Across the hall from where Flea was ministering to their mother, Matilda and Holly lay with their ears pressed over the cracks in the pine floor of their bedroom. They were listening to the conversation in the parlor below. They justified the eavesdropping with the rationale that they would be able to act in a wiser manner if they knew what Leopold and the sheriff were planning. What they heard surprised them. Newton Ludwell kept asking questions about the foreign relative, Emma Bean. His suspicions had been aroused when he'd learned Emma worked as a consultant in Washington. He became even more suspicious when he learned her work was confidential. By some perverse twist of logic, he combined this knowledge with Leopold's suggestion that Archibald had been kidnapped and developed a theory connecting the boy's disappearance with the actions of a terrorist group.

"Nonsense." Holly lifted her ear from the floor and grinned.

"Most definitely," Matilda agreed.

"They'll never figure it out. Think we should tell them?"

"Probably. We can't get to the rug now, not with Flea in the room. And it would do no good showing up at the gate empty-handed. The kidnapper would kill Archibald if I did that."

"Bingo!" Holly lit with sudden insight. "Let's give him one of my quilted saddle-blankets. They look just like oriental rugs. At least they do to me. Unless he's smarter than you described him, he'd never know the difference at night."

Matilda reflected a moment, then for the first time since much earlier in the day, she smiled. "Holly, you may actually have something there. It might work."

Leopold and Henry listened politely as Newton expounded his ridiculous theory that Archibald had been snatched with the intention of putting pressure on Emma Bean, who would then be used to extract concessions from the U.S. government. He said it was unfortunate, but quite likely the terrorists would dispose of the boy after he was no longer useful. "Your son is just a pawn in a chess match as far as those terrorists are concerned," Newton explained. Then, perhaps hoping to soften the blow, he added, "Henry, I hope I'm wrong."

"You are," Henry said gruffly. "I couldn't think of a dumber explanation if I tried."

"I understand your anger," said Newton. "The families of the victim are often bitter."

Leopold saw Henry's muscles tighten, and decided to intercede. He rose from his seat. "Newton, I suggest that you head back to Binkerton and see what you can track down from there. Leave Henry and me to cover this side of the county."

"Okay, Hillacre. If you hear anything, call me," said Newton, but his words bounced off the backs of Leopold and Henry, who were already on their way out the door.

Crowley Hogget was an ugly, pernicious ignoramus, but he was not a stupid fool. At twenty before midnight he parked the Jeep in the woods on the side of the road a half mile from the gravel driveway leading to Dither Farm. He wanted to arrive early at the gate, in time to scout for traps. Archibald was under a tarp in the backseat. His wrists were bound with twine, his mouth was sealed with duct tape, and he was tethered around the waist with a nylon cord. Crowley cut several branches, which he tossed over the Jeep, then reached through the rear window of the vehicle and grabbed Archibald by the ear. He tugged, twisted, and hissed into the ear, "This is it, squirt. Keep up with me or I'll drag you on your stomach through these woods."

Archibald did his best to keep up with Crowley, but it was a struggle for him to maintain slack in the cord and stay on his feet. It would have been easier if his hands had been free to ward off the briars and low-hanging branches. When he did stumble, Crowley did not hesitate to yank forcefully on the cord. Poor kid, he was defenseless against the obstacles reaching out at him in the night. His tear-stained face was soon bruised and scratched in many places.

It was ten minutes before midnight when Holly and Matilda entered their parents' bedroom to check on their mother (who was in a deep sleep) and to ask Flea for permission to go outside.

"We just want to sit on the porch," said Matilda.

"We can't sleep," Holly explained.

"That's understandable," Flea said. "But don't stray from the house. I want you nearby. Okay, girls?"

"Yes, Flea."

"Thank you, Flea."

As the sisters left the room, Flea mused to herself: Those innocent, sweet little angels.

Crowley stopped in the woods approximately fifty yards from the gate and tied Archibald to a pine tree. He then went and lay in the weeds near the mailbox. He could see the house two hundred yards away. There were lights on inside, and numerous vehicles parked outside. Suddenly it occurred to him that Matilda might not be able to keep the midnight appointment. But soon he heard footsteps and knew otherwise. He remained hidden and listened as the girls whispered to each other.

"I don't see him. He's not here. Let's go back."

"We can't."

"Is he really so horrible?"

"Uglier than sin."

"I hope he didn't panic and kill Archibald already."

"Don't say that."

"Sorry."

Holly and Matilda froze in their tracks when a heavy voice interjected, "You'll be sorry if you didn't bring me the flying carpet." Crowley jumped from the weeds and glared at the cowering girls.

When Holly finally caught her breath, she jabbed Matilda with an elbow and said out of the side of her mouth, "You didn't tell me it flew."

Crowley laughed. "She didn't tell you that it flies." He stepped forward with his hand out. "Give me it."

"Nope." Matilda backed away with the saddle blanket. "Not until I see my brother."

"A tough nut, eh?" Crowley smirked.

"I want to see Archibald."

"Hey, all right." Crowley was amused by Matilda's forceful manner. "Just this way. He's right over here."

Crowley led the sisters to within thirty yards of the pine tree where Archibald was tied, then stopped and pointed. Although the girls could not see the cuts and bruises on his gagged face, they could see that it was Archibald. He made a grunting noise when he saw them.

"There," said Crowley. "Now give me the carpet and I'll go. You can untie the squirt—or leave him," he added as a joke.

"All right. It's a deal," Matilda said. She stepped forward and handed Crowley the quilted saddle-blanket. Quickly both she and her sister moved toward the tree. They had gone approximately ten feet when they were stopped cold.

"Hold it or you're dead," Crowley commanded. "Before you free the runt, I want to see this thing fly."

"Excuse me?" Matilda's heart sank.

"I said, I want to see this thing fly before I give you back your brother."

"Sir, that's not the deal we made. I gave you the carpet, and you're supposed to give me Archibald."

"The deal has changed," Crowley growled. "Fly it and your brother goes free."

"I can't, sir. Not now." Matilda was apologetic. "It only flies at sunset. Remember, it was sunset when you saw us."

Crowley looked at the blanket, then studied Matilda with a raised brow. "Only works at sunset," he muttered.

"Yes, sir."

"Then what?"

"Then what, what? Sir?"

"How do you fly the thing?" Crowley grumbled.

"Well, it's easy. Really nothing to it. Simple," Matilda stalled. "Even Archibald figured it out. We had no trouble with it. Ask him." She pointed at Archibald.

"Shut up," Crowley snapped, then moved between the sisters and the pine tree. "I tell ya what—I'm going to be nice about this. I'm taking the squirt back with me tonight, and tomorrow at sunset he's going to show me how to fly this thing. If he gets it off the ground, I'll probably let him live. But it won't help to pray for him if

173

this rug is a fake. Now *shoo!*" Crowley swung the back of his hands at the girls.

"But, sir, you can't do this," Matilda began to argue.

"Hush, or I'll peel the freckles off your face."

"It's not fair." Holly stamped her foot.

Crowley withdrew a switchblade from his pocket and pointed it teasingly at the girls. "Sometimes life ain't fair." *Click* went the triggered blade. "Now scat, unless you want me to make mincemeat of your brother."

It was a long journey into the night for Henry. Time weighed on him like iron shackles. No reasoning or rationalization of the mind could free him. Although he was accompanied by Garland, Leopold, and Emmet in the cab of Garland's truck, with Jimmy, Wade, and Warren in the back, Henry felt painfully alone. It seemed to him his soul had abandoned him on a dark lane in the backwoods of Willow County. Or if not his soul, his ability to hope. There was nothing to build on; no hints, no clues, no facts. That Archibald was missing was all he knew. Everything else was W's: why, what, when, where, and weary for wondering. The questions cycled through his head until he was empty of all emotion except anger. Ironically, he concluded as Crowley had earlier informed his daughters: "Sometimes life ain't fair."

Very late that night, in the darkest hour before dawn, after driving many miles and knocking on many doors, Garland turned right on Route 628 and drove into the parking lot at Aylor's Store. As he parked, the truck headlights hit the plate-glass windows in the front of the store and illuminated the porch like a stage. Silhouetted in the window was Carl Plummers. He was bent forward like Rodin's *Thinker*, with his chin resting upon clasped hands. For an instant Henry was able to trade his own pain for compassion. "Poor Carl. I bet he's taking this mighty hard."

Carl was indeed taking it hard. Everyone was. Especially

Leopold. He would not allow a second to pass unresolved. As the others got out of the pickup and followed Jimmy into the store, the author of *The Comprehensive Guide* sat alone at the mossy base of an oak tree and meditated. He wanted to give his inner voice an opportunity to speak. Given the proper conditions, he knew from experience, the voice would come to life. He trusted it to help him now. After all, it had initially sounded the alarm and warned him of foul play. Leopold reminded himself of a couple of sentences he had recently written: "There is a fine line between thinking and listening to your own thoughts. It is this line that separates the intellect from the psychic."

Just let it flow, quit trying, he advised himself.

And so he did . . . absorbing the darkness, feeling the workings of time. He did not notice the bark of the tree pressing against his back, or the acorn in the moss beneath his buttocks. He was aware only of the master clock unwinding. Tick, tick, tick, it kept pace with his beating heart. Eventually he began to drift into that realm between consciousness and sleep. Tick, tick. Then he heard it—a faint voice speaking from deep within him. It sounded like a woman's voice. "Matilda found the missing piece," it said.

"What?" Leopold whispered.

Silence was the reply. Silence and darkness, and the tick, tick, tick of time.

seventeen

TUESDAY WAS A DAY for the record books.

Considering that he had been abducted, had his freedom dangled before him then postponed, and afterward been bullied back to Hogget's hideout, Archibald managed to get in a surprisingly good night's sleep on Monday. That is one of the great advantages of being a kid. His left ankle had been tied to a door frame, his hands were bound, and he was in the same room with the cretin Crowley, yet he had a blanket and was permitted to use the burlap sack as a pillow. It could have been worse, he reasoned. The tape had been removed from his mouth, no one tortured him, and now that he understood why he had been kidnapped, he was no longer so panic-stricken. He trusted Matilda and Holly to do their best to save his hide.

It was just after sunup when Archibald awoke to the smell of smoke. He could see through the open back door of the hut to where Acorn was hunched over a small fire, watching an aluminum pot. When the water in it began to boil, Acorn added a handful of ground coffee. Archibald sat up and sniffed at the strong smell invading the room where he was tied. Acorn saw the movement inside the hut and turned to observe Archibald waving his nose back and forth. Acorn chuckled quietly and allowed his better nature to rise. He signaled the captive with a clucking sound, then put a finger to his lips for silence. After Archibald indicated with a nod that he understood, Acorn crept forward and untied the nylon cord from the door frame. He also undid the twine around Archibald's wrists. Then, without a word, Acorn crawled back to the area of the fire and attached the cord to a nearby slab of broken concrete. Archibald joined him and watched with growing bemusement as Acorn filled two tin cups with black brew, added four packs of sugar to each cup, and kindly offered him one to drink. "Gee, thanks," Archibald whispered.

"No problem," replied Acorn. "I make it kinda strong and sweet. Hope that's the way you take your coffee."

"I don't know. I've never had any before."

"You're shushing me." Acorn was astonished.

"I'm not." Archibald sipped from the cup. "This is the first time for me."

"Wow. Your parents must be pretty mean."

"No, they're nice. I've just never asked for coffee."

"Oh."

"But I will when I'm free again."

In the next moment Bart emerged from his sleeping place in the woods. He was barefoot. His clothes were rumpled. "How ya'll doing this morning?" he asked. "Any coffee left?"

"Yep." Acorn nodded toward the aluminum pot.

"Mind if I get a cup?"

"Help yourself."

Bart stooped and poured himself a large cup of coffee. "Is the boss awake?" he asked after taking a sip.

"Listen," said Acorn.

"Is he snoring or what?" Bart smiled. "How'd you sleep?"

"Pretty good, I reckon," said Acorn.

Archibald, who had thus far been silent, burst into the conversation. "Wow, I really like this stuff. No wonder it's so popular with grownups. Ha. I think I'll get a refill. Say, are you guys brothers? I've got a brother too. He has a monkey. Hey, you don't mind if I exercise, do you? I won't try to escape."

"Go ahead." Acorn grinned.

"Thanks a million." Archibald leaped to his feet and began doing jumping jacks.

"Does he look wound up to you?" asked Bart.

"Seems to like the way I make coffee," remarked Acorn.

While Archibald was flapping around in the sheer joy of movement, his mother was in bed, slowly stretching her limbs and wiggling her extremities. She was beginning to wake from a deep, valerian-induced sleep. Her husband had just come into the room and flopped in bed beside her. He was exhausted, having been up all night searching for their son. As she rolled her head on the pillow and blinked open her eyes, she was aware of the tenuous remnants of a dream slipping from her conscious mind. She had just seen Archibald. He had been wearing his favorite red shorts. He was dancing. He seemed happy. There was smoke in the air. Then the dream changed and suddenly Archibald was attired in his Sunday suit. He was moving without walking. He appeared to be looking through a crowd. Clementine felt as though he was looking at her. He grinned wildly, court-rolled his right arm, opened his hand, and bowed elegantly at the waist. There was confetti in the air. Drums. Trumpets.

Clementine elevated herself onto her elbows. The dream was gone. She heard Henry breathing heavily. When she placed a hand on his chest, he mumbled to her, "We looked everywhere. Nothing.

I don't know what to tell you. Right now I need a little nap."

"Henry." Clementine rolled against Henry and laid her head close to his. "I just had an incredible dream. I can't explain it, but I think Archibald is safe. I have a feeling he will be home soon."

"That's strange. Just a minute ago Leopold said almost the same thing to me." Henry snuggled with his wife. "He said he was sure no harm had come to Archibald yet."

"Yet?"

"That's what Leopold said."

"It must be true." Clementine rolled onto her back and gazed at the ceiling. "I must remember I believe that."

"Bzzz." Henry drifted into a patch of much-needed sleep.

Matilda snapped awake when she heard Leopold say her name. He was standing in the bedroom doorway. "Wake up. I need some facts from you."

Matilda raised herself to an upright position. "Leopold. I'm so glad you're here. I've got something I want to tell you."

"I was afraid you might." The old man frowned.

"Archibald has been kidnapped."

"I knew it." Leopold frowned further.

"How did you know?" Matilda looked quizzically at Leopold.

"Never mind how I knew. How did you know?"

"It's complicated. A lot has happened these past few days. It'll take a while to tell you everything."

"I'm here to listen." Leopold crossed his arms.

Matilda shrugged. "All right. Let me see. I'm not sure exactly where to start."

"If you know anything about a missing piece, begin with that." Leopold's voice carried the harsh edge of a long night. "And stick to the issue. I'm not in the mood for a lot of chitchat."

"Please don't be angry, Leopold." Matilda's voice cracked. "I'm pretty upset already."

"We're all upset. How do you know it was a kidnapping?"

"I know . . . because I spoke with the kidnapper last night. He's a big, mean, ugly man. He said he would slit Archibald's throat if I blabbed to any adults."

"Last night?"

"Yes."

"You know who he is?"

"Not his name. I've seen him."

"And Archibald?"

"I saw him, too, last night. Out by the front gate. He was tied to a pine tree. I didn't get to talk to him."

Leopold pointed at Holly. "What does she know?"

"About half of what I do," answered Matilda.

"Get dressed and meet me downstairs," Leopold ordered. "You are going to present me with all the facts."

"I'll be glad to," Matilda replied with alacrity. She felt a tremendous relief now that she knew Leopold would be sharing her burden.

When Matilda came down the steps, Leopold was waiting by the back door. He led her outside, where they then walked to the apple orchard. It was a quiet morning. Leopold paused to admire the view from the ridge, then crossed his arms and instructed Matilda to divulge all she knew about Archibald's disappearance.

Matilda poured out her guts. Having Leopold's ear gave her confidence. Who else in all the world (besides Great-Aunt Emma, of course) would or could believe what she was saying? She knew that if anyone was capable of unraveling the snarl of circumstances closing in on her, it had to be Leopold. He listened patiently, occasionally huffing or moaning, but never interrupting. Finally she concluded, "And here we are."

Leopold did not speak for the longest moment. His lips were pursed, and the lines in his weathered face were drawn in deep reflection. It was impossible to know from his expression what he was thinking. Matilda hung her head and waited with the shame of the guilty. She had deceived her parents and thieved from her great-aunt. And now her brother and half of Willow County were suffering from the consequences of her crime.

Leopold pried himself from his reflections and cleared his throat. In a surprising gesture, he patted Matilda on the back with a firm yet gentle hand, and winked conspiratorially. "I believe your aunt would appreciate it if we kept the carpet a secret. You must make Holly swear to silence. I'll figure out something to tell your parents. Your father, by the way, has had dealings with the kidnapper before."

"You know who he is?"

"I have a solid hunch."

"Oh, Leopold." Matilda hugged her elderly friend around the waist. "I don't know what I'd do without you."

"Save the gratitude. Archibald isn't out of the woods yet. We have only a dozen or so hours in which to find him."

Tuesday morning was eventful in more places than Willow County. When Emma Bean arrived at the classroom where she had been holding her Sharp sessions, she found a letter awaiting her that officially terminated her consulting contract. She would receive full payment for her work, but her services were no longer required. Although there was no explanation for her dismissal, the reason was obvious. "Guess I was too honest about the Zandinski Box," she muttered to herself, then let out a whoop of joy. Happily she gathered her teaching materials from the room, and without sparing Washington so much as a sentimental thought, she began planning her departure from town.

At the same time that Emma was arranging to check out of her room at the Watergate, her ex-project coordinator, Simmons, was fielding a telephone call that had been patched through to his desk by a beleagured operator working the White House switchboard.

The call was from Sheriff Newton Ludwell, of Willow County. He was insisting on speaking with an upper-echelon official who could personally relay his report to the President. This was his eighth call to the White House. Throughout the night and early-morning hours, he had left urgent messages with a clerk at the FBI, on answering machines at the State Department, and with numerous operators at the White House. He claimed that he, a duly (some say dully) elected official of the town of Binkerton, Virginia, wanted to report an incident of vital national interest, and he wanted to report it to someone in the Presidential Cabinet.

Simmons spoke with the agitated operator and then clicked onto the line. "The White House. Your conversation is being recorded. I understand you have a message for the President. What is it?"

"Who is this?"

"Simmons. Who are you?"

"My name is Newton Ludwell. I am the highest-ranking law officer in the town of Binkerton. Who are you?"

"Simmons. I'm on the President's team. What is this about?"

"A possible terrorist threat."

"To whom? Who are the terrorists?"

"If I knew who they were, I'd arrest them," quipped Newton.

"What is the threat?"

"Well, they haven't made one yet. Not exactly. I am calling to alert you before they do."

"Better explain," said Simmons.

Newton proceeded to lay out his theory about Archibald's kidnapping being part of a plot to extort political concessions from the government. It was by pure coincidence that Simmons happened to know Emma Bean, although he did not inform Newton of the fact. He simply waited until the obviously deluded sheriff finished talking, then responded, "I see. And you thought this up by yourself?"

"Yes," Newton said proudly. "I'm keen on espionage."

Simmons decided to humor the man from Binkerton. "Thank you for the report. For now I believe it would be best to keep this quiet and wait for the terrorists to make their demands. I will look into the matter from here. Don't call me again unless they contact you. Got that?"

"Roger, Simmons."

"I will let you know if and when I discover something."

"Right-o," said Newton. "A real pleasure working with you." Newton hung up the phone and leaned back in his swivel chair. He felt terrific. He had spoken with the White House. He was playing with the big boys now.

During the course of Tuesday morning, word that a child was missing spread rapidly through the town of Binkerton. An aura of uncertainty soon fell over the planned festivities. "It's things like this that will dampen the spirit of a parade quicker than a rainstorm," remarked one concerned merchant. Many of the local residents knew the Dither name—Clementine had dominated the Pie and Pastry Division of the Culinary Competition for years—but few Binkertonians were personally acquainted with Archibald. Eugenna White, director of the Women's Auxiliary to the Binkerton Volunteer Fire Department, and one of the principal organizers of the BIF, was afraid rumors of the kidnapping might spread statewide and discourage tourists from attending the festival. Since Binkerton's civic groups had grown to rely on the annual influx of revenue, she felt compelled to belittle the significance of the incident. She launched a counter-rumor that Archibald Dither was a habitual runaway and was probably off on one of his usual jaunts. Yet few in Binkerton were misled. They knew how low Eugenna would stoop.

Unfortunately for the younger population, mass paranoia settled upon the town. Many children found themselves tied and tethered, just like Archibald, or made to wear bells and restricted to their yards. One of the youngsters adversely affected by the news was

Contessa Cunningham. She was carrying an armload of prizes from the truck to her father's booth when he casually mentioned, "They say a boy has been kidnapped."

"A boy? From where, Binkerton?" asked Contessa.

"No, from over around Aylor's Store," answered her father.

A stuffed zebra fell from her arms to the floor. She paused before picking it up. "Who? Do you know?"

"Something Dither. I forget. I believe someone might have said his name was—" Mike Cunningham stopped speaking and dove to catch his daughter before she hit the pavilion floor.

It was after ten A.M. when the ursine Crowley Hogget stretched his limbs and greeted the day with a growl. He had been dreaming of the great wealth he would have after the sale of the flying carpet. He rolled onto his side and was about to return to his dream when he cast a groggy eye toward the captive's corner. He came wide awake when he saw it was empty. He jumped to his feet. There was an odd noise coming from outside the hut. He yanked on a pair of canvas pants and stumbled into the open.

"Morning, boss." Acorn snapped to attention. "Letting the kid get some exercise. He's been at it an hour and a half already."

"Do you believe he's never had coffee before?" asked Bart.

Crowley grumbled, "I believe that you two can't get any dumber than you are. From now on, you'll just get older." Crowley whirled on his heels and shouted at Archibald, "Hey, jumping beans! Quit flapping around. You're making me nervous."

"Sorry. Didn't mean to do that," Archibald puffed.

Back on the farm, where everyone was nervous, Holly had to restrain from spilling the beans when Clementine called her into the parlor and with teary eyes informed her that Archibald had been kidnapped. Holly was aware of an ironic twist in her role as a daughter:

She longed to take her mother in her arms and comfort her. Instead she said, "Mom, I love you."

Clementine pulled Holly close and cradled her. "I hope we get him back in time for the parade on Saturday."

"It's okay if we don't. There'll be other parades. I just hope the kidnapper doesn't slit his throat."

"Holly! What a horrible thing to say. Where did you ever get an idea like that?"

"Sorry, Mom. I've been reading too many Westerns, I guess."

At about noon on that historically hectic Tuesday, Millie Ross and Alice Aylor stopped by Dither Farm to check on Clementine. They were on their way to Binkerton, and they offered to deliver Clementine's pies to the pavilion before the entry deadline at three. The Pie and Pastry Division was to be judged that evening. Clementine was reluctant to enter her pies in the contest. She felt that under the circumstances it was not proper. "Also," she added, "if I won, people might think it was because the judges felt sorry for me."

"Nonsense," said Alice. "All entries are tagged with numbers. No one knows who baked what until after the winners are announced on Thursday." She nodded toward the kitchen. "Come on, Millie, let's take those prizewinning confections to town."

eighteen

THE MEN WAITING at Aylor's Store at two o'clock on Tuesday afternoon almost did not recognize their good friend Henry when he entered with Leopold. They knew who he was, of course; but they had never seen him in such a state. Earlier, when he learned from Leopold that Crowley Hogget had kidnapped his son, Henry's face had contracted into a tight, restrictive mask through which he could barely speak. His friends were stunned, unsure of how to greet him. For an awkward moment Jimmy Aylor, Carl Plummers, Wade Butcher, Garland Barlow, Felton Fibbs, John Washington, Buddy Breedon, and Flugga Gibson stood silently, expectantly, and waited. Henry's shoulders and neck muscles rippled with tension as he glared at the men. A witness might have wondered if the eight of them could have subdued him if he'd attacked. But he did not attack. He just fumed and quivered.

"Maybe I better explain." Leopold stepped forward. "We have recently learned that Crowley Hogget has kidnapped Archibald."

"What! How do you know that?"

"Holly and Matilda saw him. He wanted a ransom."

"Why, that no-good, greasy, ignorant skunk!" Wade jumped into a fighting position. He was ready to roll.

"Where do we find him?" asked Garland.

"I don't know," said Leopold. "But we better locate him before he does something stupid."

"Grrr." Henry tried to speak and failed.

"Anyone know where Crowley hangs his hat?" asked Wade.

"The Hot Spot," suggested Felton.

"Yeah, we know that, but he wouldn't be there with Archibald," said Buddy. "Though maybe he has a place near Binkerton somewhere. Least that's where I usually see him."

"He drives a beat-up old Jeep. The lout almost ran me into a ditch last week," said Flugga Gibson.

"Grrr," interjected Henry.

"Let's go look in Binkerton," said Jimmy.

"What about Sheriff Ludwell's instructions for us to wait here?" asked John.

"Forget him," huffed Wade.

"I'll second that." Garland hopped down from the counter and stood in the center of the group. "Right now Newton is sitting over in Binkerton on his precious bum, straining that squash he has for a brain, trying to figure out a way to turn this to his advantage. We don't need him."

"That's right," said Felton. "He didn't even show up when the boys were lost in the swamp. And they got out okay."

"Grrr," said Henry.

The men decided to split up into three teams. Henry, Jimmy, and Leopold rode with Garland. Henry sat up front in the middle, with Leopold by the passenger window and Jimmy in the back. As they traveled the blacktop miles of Route 631 heading west into Binkerton, Henry slowly regained a modicum of self-control.

Although he still could not speak in complete sentences, he was able to articulate fragments of thought. He said things like, "Get him. Crush his head. That toad."

Leopold alone understood they were entered in a race with time . . . a race that presumably would end at sunset. Earlier, when questioned by the men, he had given them the same scant set of facts he had given Clementine and Henry: Crowley Hogget had contacted Matilda and offered to trade Archibald for a valuable Persian carpet that Clementine's aunt had left at Dither Farm. "No," he answered when Jimmy asked. "I can't say how Crowley knew about the carpet, or why he would want it."

"Do you know why Matilda waited a day before she told you?" asked Garland.

"She was frightened. Crowley threatened to kill Archibald if she told anybody," explained Leopold.

"When and how did he want to make the switch?" asked Garland.

"Matilda didn't know," Leopold, going against the grain of his character, lied. "She said he got mad and disappeared when she told him she didn't know what he was talking about."

During the anxiety-ridden hours of Tuesday, when Clementine was not sitting in her bedroom surrounded by Holly, Matilda, Emmet, and Warren, she would venture downstairs to the parlor to receive the various members of the community who came by the farm to express their sympathy. Flea appointed herself protector. A mother goose could not have done a better job of establishing a buffer zone between Clementine and some of the more pessimistic, hysterical visitors. For example, when Missy Hobkins began to sob and share a story she had once read, about a boy who had been kidnapped and reared by coyotes, Flea interceded, and sort of flapped and pecked Missy into the next room.

Clementine hardly noticed what Flea was doing for her, and was only vaguely aware of the people passing through her home. Aside from the fears she felt for Archibald, her awareness was limited to her other children, now safe at her side. She saw, perhaps for the first time, that Holly was rapidly growing into a young woman. Her behavior since the beginning of the crisis had been that of a mature, considerate, older daughter. Her presence had done much to mitigate Clementine's fears. Emmet was also a reassuring force. He comported himself with a brave, confident manner. Clementine decided Emmet was probably more resourceful than the average adult. It was Matilda who worried her. It was unlike Matilda to be weak with emotion; usually she was so well balanced. Yet throughout this tragic Tuesday she had been nearly dysfunctional with grief. At the moment she was cuddled in a corner beside Goosebumps. Her chin rested on her chest and her red eyebrows were furrowed in a downcast **V**. It was obvious to Clementine that Matilda was overcome by fear. (Actually Matilda was too busy experiencing remorse to be afraid. She had begun serving time on a self-imposed penitence. Holly had been right. Suicide was the coward's way out. Instead, Matilda had sentenced herself to a year of silence for each of her major sins. By her own count she did not expect to speak again until she was fourteen. Even then, she knew, she would not be redeemed if any harm befell her brother.) Though Clementine was able to make these observations about her older children, they were thoughts that arose far from her heart and all that really mattered. To what she could currently see and feel, the only relevance in the world was Archibald.

At two thirty-three on that tense Tuesday afternoon, a sleek government sedan came rolling down the driveway and stopped at the house. A uniformed chauffeur jumped out and opened the rear door. In the next instant one of Emma Bean's shapely legs appeared. It was immediately followed by the rest of her. After the chauffeur retrieved her bags from the trunk, she informed him that she had

189

been fired that morning and would have no further need of his services. A charming fellow, he was not upset by the news. He smiled, tipped his hat, then got back in the car and drove away. When Emma turned toward the house, she found herself greeted by a very grim group indeed. No psychic skills were necessary for her to sense that life was amiss on Dither Farm.

Garland had been driving steadily for two hours, except for a few quick stops to call into the woods or to investigate an abandoned building. Conversation in the cab of the truck was all but nonexistent. Mostly the men sat and asked themselves, Where? Intermittently Henry would come out with a defamatory remark about Crowley, or Leopold would say, "Let's look there," to which Garland would reply, "Okay"—but in essence the men held their tongues and worked their eyes. In the back, Jimmy did likewise. He stood with his arms on the roof of the cab and studied the countryside with the alertness of a captain sailing through pirated waters.

At about four Garland espied Newton Ludwell traveling toward them in his squad car. "Here comes Einstein," he remarked. The two vehicles stopped side by side in the road. Garland and Leopold got out to speak with the sheriff.

Newton rolled down his window and remained seated. "You guys are just burning up gas. Go on home now and get some rest."

"Say what?" Jimmy called from the back of the truck.

"I said take a break. I already sent Wade Butcher and his crew home. Y'all do the same. The Feds are working with me on the case. That's all the help I need. We'll find the boy soon enough."

"Grrr." Henry moved to climb out of the truck, but desisted at a sign from Leopold.

"The Feds," said Leopold in a cynical tone.

"That's right," replied Newton. "And we professionals do not appreciate vigilantes muddying up the waters."

"Newton . . ." Garland started to speak, then had second

thoughts. He shook his head and climbed back in the truck.

"Hillacre, you're a responsible man. Get your friends to go home. I'd hate to have to arrest them."

Leopold looked at the smug county cop with an expression that defied description. "Ludwell," he said in a voice that implied many things, "I suggest you put your car in gear and get on down the road."

Newton hesitated, then followed Leopold's sagacious advice.

After the fuss over her unexpected arrival died down, it took Emma Bean a full twenty minutes to piece together an understanding of what had occurred. Although the details were obscured by Matilda's reluctance to speak, Emma got the larger picture from Clementine and Flea. She added to it selected tidbits of input from Holly, Warren, and Emmet, then let everything meld in her imagination. After a while she had an approximate understanding of the situation. But understanding is not the same as resolving, and Emma spent the next few hours grappling with the same problem everyone else was facing.

It was five after seven when Garland's truck crossed through the open gate at Dither Farm. Clementine heard the vehicle approaching and went to stand at the back door. She could see defeat in the men's faces as they climbed out of the truck and started across the yard. Her already-sad face grew sadder.

When Henry, Jimmy, Leopold, and Garland entered the house, they were surprised to find Emma Bean in the parlor, although under the circumstances their reactions were muted. In situations such as the one at hand, social reunions weigh lightly upon the mental scales. Even Leopold accepted Emma's presence in a matter-of-fact manner. He greeted her with a casual nod, then waved Holly out of a chair and sat down. This was not the time for flirtation. Henry sank down on the sofa between Flea and Clementine, then

191

took his wife's hand in his. Garland moved behind the chair where Emma was sitting and rested his weary frame against the wall. Jimmy grabbed a footstool and pushed it into the middle of the room, sat down, and said, "We have some thinking to do."

Flea looked at Jimmy and corrected his last remark. "Not thinking. Doing. We have some doing to do."

"Yes, Flea, we do," agreed Leopold. "And I don't know if or how much anyone else is aware of it, but we must do it soon. It is imperative that we find Archibald before tonight."

"Why?" Tears fell from Clementine's face as she asked, "Why is it imperative?"

"Because none of us trust Crowley Hogget as far as we can throw him," answered Garland.

"He is a very rash man," added Jimmy.

Clementine continued to look at Leopold. "Do you know something you're not telling us?"

Pain mixed with compassion in Leopold's face as he gazed at the bereaved Clementine. Moved by the power of her grief, he was on the verge of telling her about Crowley's ultimatum when Emma Bean rose from her chair and started across the room. She stopped just outside the doorway and bent to pick up her briefcase from the outer hall. All eyes were on her as she turned to the group. "I believe there is a way we can find where Archibald is being held." Emma spoke slowly. Her eyes lingered on Leopold for a moment before she opened her briefcase and looked inside. "I *know* it is possible," she added.

"How?" The question came from Jimmy. It was echoed in whispers by both Flea and Garland.

"With this," Emma said, as she took from her briefcase and held up for all to see a Zandinski Box.

nineteen

SINCE THE MOMENT of his abduction the previous afternoon, Archibald had been given for sustenance two sardine-and-cracker sandwiches, one Moon Pie, a banana, three glasses of water, and two large cups of strong, sugary coffee. For most of Tuesday the young hostage had wiggled, jabbered, and jumped. Now, at half past six in the evening, he was suddenly out of gas. He yawned an extended yawn, then stretched out on the hard ground. With the crook of his arm shielding his eyes from the descending sun, he sank into a deep, satisfying sleep.

Soon after Archibald drifted off, with approximately an hour remaining before sunset, Crowley withdrew Holly's quilted saddle-blanket from beneath his cot and unfolded it on the floor. This was his fifth inspection of the blanket. On Sunday, when the kids had flown by him, he had not gotten a good look at the magic carpet; thus he had only instincts with which to judge the blanket. And these, by his nature, were suspicious. He could not explain it, but he had a feeling this was not the rug he'd bargained for. Even Bart, never known for his astuteness, had remarked, "I wonder if all magic carpets look so much like horse blankets?" So now, when Crowley picked from the rug what appeared to be a white horse-hair, it struck him that he had been hornswoggled. He grabbed the blanket and put it to his nose. It smelled of horse. His face turned a shade of purple where he slapped himself on the forehead. On the brink of internal combustion, he screamed, "Acorn, Bart! Rouse that runt and bring him in here."

Acorn rushed over to the sleeping captive and tapped him on the shoulder. "Okay, mister squirt. Wake up."

Archibald did not stir. Acorn tapped him again, then rocked him side to side. Still Archibald did not open his eyes. Acorn slapped him across the cheek gently and pleaded, "Quit fooling around now. The boss is going to go berserk."

Still nothing.

"Want me to tell the boss we can't wake him?" asked Bart, but there was no need. Crowley was on his way outside.

Archibald happened to be dreaming of buttered pancakes with strawberry jam when he felt the impact of a boot stinging his bottom side. Startled awake, he forgot where he was for an instant. It all came back like a nightmare when he saw Crowley's ugly face staring down at him. In one hand he held a cup of cold coffee. In the other he held the saddle blanket. Archibald felt his nerve rising with his temper. "Chiggers. Ya didn't have to break my tailbone," he scolded his captor.

Crowley handed him the coffee. "Shut up and drink this, or I'll break your head."

Archibald declined. "I've had enough for one day."

"Drink it," Crowley growled. "I want you wide awake when I clean your ears with this rag your sister pawned off on me."

Archibald stood and rubbed his sore buttocks. Needing time to think, he accepted the coffee from Crowley and drank several swallows. He nodded at Acorn. "Just the way I like it." He took another sip. Crowley began to foam about the mouth. Archibald sensed that Crowley was near the end of his patience. "What rag?" he asked.

"You know what I'm talking about," Crowley snorted. "Your cheating sister pulled a fast one on me."

"She wouldn't do that. Not Matilda," Archibald said in a tone of disbelief.

"Oh yeah? Look at this." Crowley unfurled the blanket. "I couldn't see very good the other night, but I can see right now."

"What?" Archibald gulped more coffee.

"That is a no-good horse blanket, that's what," Crowley hollered into Archibald's face. "I even found a hair on it."

"You did?" Archibald pretended to be shocked.

"Here." Crowley pulled a white hair from his top pocket and handed it to Archibald. "If this ain't a horse hair, what is it?"

Archibald laid the hair in his palm and examined it with the scrutiny of a molecular biologist studying a strand of DNA. It was obviously from Dan's coat. Nevertheless, he rolled it over, flipped it end to end, then tested it for tensile strength. This seemed to tell him something. He handed the hair back to Crowley and enjoyed another sip of coffee. Then he cleared his throat and addressed Crowley in a scholarly fashion. "That, sir, is quite apparently the hair of an albino camel. The previous owner of this magic blan— carpet lived in the Sahara Desert on a farm with lots and lots of camels."

"Wow." Acorn could not suppress his awe.

Crowley glared at his diminutive hostage with the meanest, most despicable look he could muster. Ugly on ugly—the look sent shivers of fear through Acorn and Bart, but Archibald did not cower. He met Crowley's glare with a look that only someone who has successfully invoked the *hoche haumdoo* chant can attain. Like two boxers before a match, they eye-wrestled. Eventually Crowley blinked. "Okay, you little weasel. I'll be sporting about this. The sun will set in roughly forty-five minutes. I'm going to let you prove me wrong. But if you don't, and this *thing* won't fly, then I'm going to stuff it down your throat."

"Don't worry," Archibald said with confidence. "But we will need to find an open area for takeoff. Best if it's on a hill. Too dangerous trying to navigate out of bottomland like this."

"How about the area around the sawdust pile?" Bart asked.

"Perfect," said Crowley. "We'll go there when the time comes."

Although the group gathered in the parlor was desperately open-minded and willing to try anything to save Archibald, and though they held Emma in high esteem, they could not help but harbor a degree of skepticism about the Box. Even Leopold, a student of the unknown, suffered a tinge of reservation about the psychic booster. Were it not for Emma's endorsement, not one of them would have given it a try. She knew it was necessary that the user of the Box believe in it completely for it to work, so she did not qualify her pitch with any disclaimers. "I know it sounds kooky," she admitted. "But I promise you the Zandinski Box does work. And right now we need something that works."

Clementine, who knew that Emma understood much about the hidden world, was the first to accede. She scooted forward on the sofa and held out her open hands. "I will try it, Emma. Just show me what to do."

Emma handed Clementine the Box and instructed her to peer through the built-in magnifying glass. "On the back panel are nine small mirrors. Look at them and think about Archibald. The mirrors will blend into a screen, or field, that will catch your mental vibrations and reflect them back to you in the form of images."

"Then what?"

"Then you will see."

"Like this?" Clementine held the Box up to her eyes.

"Yes. Go ahead," Emma said softly. "While she is looking, the rest of us should concentrate on seeing Archibald. Pretend he is here in front of you."

A hush fell over the parlor as Clementine began to pour her thoughts into the Zandinski Box. She seemed so needy, so sincere, that all present in the parlor could not help but align themselves in emotional empathy. The task was not to question whether the Box would fail or succeed, but to locate Archibald. Each person, in his or her own manner, did as Emma requested, and concentrated on visualizing Archibald while Clementine looked into the Box. After a silent, timeless span, she bolted erect and gasped. Then she lowered the Box from her eyes and dropped her gaze to the floor.

"What?" Henry said.

There was an introspective quality to Clementine's gaze as she lifted it even with Henry's. Her voice sounded small as she told him, "It was exactly the same as my dream this morning. I saw Archibald dressed up in his best suit of clothes. He was waving at me. It was strange."

"Where? Where was he?" asked Henry.

"I don't know. I couldn't see."

"This is ridiculous," sighed Jimmy. "We're wasting time."

Emma glanced at Jimmy. Her eyes said that he was free to believe whatever he wished but not to influence the others.

Leopold leaned forward and clapped his hands. "Emma, should she try it again? Or would it work better if you tried it? You know Archibald. You've used the Box before."

Emma shook her head no. "If Archibald is being held here in the county, I think it is important for the user to know the lay of the land well. Even if I did see him, it wouldn't help."

"You do it, Leopold," urged Garland. "No one knows the county better than you. Besides, you're good at these things."

"Me?" Leopold seemed surprised.

"Yes," Emma agreed. "I would think you have the talent."

"Please, someone do it," Flea said nervously.

Clementine handed the Box to Leopold. Although he accepted it with his hands, his attention was directed at the wall clock. Less than thirty minutes remained before sunset. He heaved a sigh of resignation and looked at the Box with a detached air.

"Go ahead, Leopold," Garland said encouragingly.

"No," Leopold answered with clear conviction, holding out the Zandinski Box. "Henry is the one for whom this will work."

"I don't know about that," Henry muttered.

"I do," Leopold said authoritatively. "And we do not have time for a debate."

"Someone try it." Jimmy threw up his hands.

"He's right." Emma sided with Leopold. "Henry, just relax and see if you can see anything."

"Go ahead, honey."

"Yeah, go on, Dad."

Henry shrugged and reluctantly took the Box from Leopold. He held it with both hands and peered through the rounded opening. At first all he could see were nine separate reflections of his magnified eye. But he ignored this distraction and put his energy into thinking about Archibald. Soon the mirrors began to blend into a single field of perception unified in a milky cloud. Then slowly an image emerged. Henry recognized it as part of the past. He saw himself as a younger man, standing by a large pile of logs. Someone handed him a check, which he put in his pocket. In the background he could see his truck. Then the image began to fade, and soon there was only his eye in the mirrors. Disappointment haunted his features as he lowered the Box and shook his head. "No sign of Archibald. All I saw was me a long time ago, back when I sold some timber to Kurt Stoke."

"Where were you when you sold the timber?" asked Emma.

"At his sawmill."

"Strange you'd see that," said Garland. "Kurt shut down his sawmill nearly ten years ago."

"A perfect spot for a hideout," observed Flea.

"Good thinking, Flea! That's the ticket." Leopold leaped to his feet and shouted, "Come on, fellows, let's go!"

"Coming," cried Jimmy.

"Hurry," shouted Flea.

"Grrr," revved Henry as he chased behind his friends.

It was a typical summer evening, with temperatures in the low eighties. A thin haze diminished the brilliance of the sun as it sank toward its appointment in the west. Yet on the ground, there was nothing hazy or diminished about Archibald as he marched toward his appointment by the sawdust pile. He charged forward with swinging arms and a bouncing step, as if he could not wait to arrive and show Crowley who was boss. If he was bluffing, he was bluffing well. "You'll love flying this baby," Archibald told his captor. "Nothing else like it. Oh, you might get giddy while we're gaining altitude—that's only natural—but once we're airborne, you'll feel free as a bird. It's beautiful. The views are absolutely magnificent. Way better than in an airplane."

"SHUT UP!" Crowley screamed.

"It's the coffee," remarked Acorn.

"Excuse me," Archibald apologized. "I was just trying to prepare you."

Crowley reached over and grabbed Archibald by the ear. He twisted it as he spoke. "I'll prepare you for supper if you don't shut your trap. The only time you're allowed to speak is when I ask you a question. Got that?"

"Yes, sir. I understand, sir. You won't hear another peep out of me. I won't say another word. Not under any cir—"

"Hush!" Crowley let go of the ear and swiped at Archibald.

Henry and Jimmy held tightly to the rails in the rear of the truck and Leopold propped his hands against the dash as Garland stuck the pedal to the metal. In ten minutes they traveled the twelve miles between the farm and the turnoff to Stoke's derelict sawmill, located three miles east of Binkerton. Twice the truck skidded sideways around curves, yet no one had called for Garland to slow down.

Leopold swung open the passenger door and hopped out of the truck before it came to a complete stop in a ditch on the side of the logging trail leading through the woods to the old sawmill. The others were quick to follow on his heels. Heedless of the brambles, briars, and brush in the trail, Henry charged forward with the determination of a Sherman tank. Jimmy called to him, "Henry, as much noise as you're making we couldn't sneak up on a football game."

"Grrr," responded Henry, although he did adjust the manner of his advance. Instead of crashing through everything, he spun around, leaped over, or darted by the obstacles.

With his keen woodsman's eye, Leopold soon spotted a barely perceptible break on the left side of the trail. He did not tarry. "This way," he said, before disappearing into the woods. The others struggled to stay close. They were amazed to see the old man move so fast. (They were not aware, as was Leopold, of the deadline at sunset, in seven minutes.) Suddenly Leopold halted in his tracks and signaled with a raised hand for the men to stop. Two hundred yards in the distance was the old sawmill office. Parked nearby in the brush was Hogget's Jeep. Leopold wanted to gather the men and formulate a strategy, but Henry bolted past him in a flash. Garland, Jimmy, and Leopold rushed to catch up.

The door gave way under Henry's shoulder as he charged into the empty hut.

Leopold, Garland, and Jimmy arrived ten seconds behind Henry and found him standing with tears in his eyes. Not one of them could think of what to say.

They didn't know it, but at that moment Archibald was standing on a hilltop a mere eighth of a mile away. At his feet was Holly's quilted saddle-blanket. Crowley, Acorn, and Bart were listening to the concluding remarks of an introductory course he was giving them on the proper techniques of operating a flying carpet. "Then, when we want to come down, we just stare at the place we want to be and the carpet will land. It's simple, really," Archibald explained. "And look, perfect timing. The sun is starting to set." He smiled at Crowley. "Now I will perform the ceremonial ritual, and then we will say the chant together."

"Ceremonial ritual? You didn't say nothing about any ritual," Crowley growled. "Quit stalling."

"Oh, I must have forgotten. It's the most important part. It's . . . like a rain dance. Sort of a jig to wake up the spirits," Archibald said. And then, without further ado, he wiggled his ears, wobbled his elbows, and threw himself into a fevered rendition of his famous chicken dance.

Garland strode forward and put an arm around Henry. He was preparing to say a few consoling words when suddenly his ears pricked at a distant sound. "What's that?" he asked.

"Shhh."

"What is it?"

"It's . . . it's laughter," said Leopold.

"Listen."

Clearly now, the men heard the sounds of unrestrained mirth.

"Ha-haa-haha heeeha. Is that, OH MY, funny or what?" Bart guffawed out of control. "Hahaha-heee."

"Ho ho hihumheeYeehardy ha." Acorn fell to the ground in a fit of glee.

"St-st-st-stop it, kid. Hhmmm ha whoo. Hoohoh. You're making me maaad. Oh ho aieee." Even the mean-spirited Crowley could not stop himself from laughing.

Back at the hut Leopold suddenly understood. "Archibald has the chicken dance working."

"Grrr." Henry roared through the back door of the hut and sprinted up the hill. Archibald was the first to glimpse his father streaking toward them. He was so relieved, he stopped dancing. This gave Crowley a chance to catch his breath and turn. It was too late. Henry Dither had pounced. He clenched Crowley by the scruff of the neck with one hand, and with the other he grabbed him by the seat of the pants. "Grrr," Henry growled as he hoisted the ugly brute over his head and hurled him toward the sawdust pile.

Acorn and Bart were stupefied as they watched their uncle zip through the air in a rising arc, then pass over the top of the pile and sail from view.

"Good going, Dad!" cheered Archibald.

"Son!" said Henry as he lifted the boy into his arms.

PART FOUR

twenty

NEWS OF ARCHIBALD'S rescue sent a tidal wave of relief surging through Willow and King counties. Everyone in its path was doused with renewed faith in the inevitability of goodness over evil. No one likes a kidnapper. The only people not relieved were Sheriff Newton Ludwell and Crowley Hogget. The sheriff was embarrassed (he should have been ashamed) because a capital crime had finally been perpetrated in his jurisdiction, and he had played no part in bringing the criminal to justice. Oh, he implied that he deserved some credit for calling in the Feds, but the only person who even pretended to agree with him on that account was Simmons, in Washington. "Score another one for the law. Case closed," he responded when Newton reached him by telephone.

Henry had thrown Crowley so far, he had a head start on the men and got away until the next day, when he was nabbed at the bus station in Bricksburg. A criminal psychologist happened to be present when Crowley was hauled into the Bricksburg jail. He listened to Crowley rant about a flying carpet and a wild man in the woods. He promptly diagnosed the bullying lout as a paranoid psychotic, and ordered that he be strapped into a straightjacket and locked up in an insane asylum.

Clementine and Henry felt such a surge of relief after Archibald's rescue, they could hardly stop smiling long enough to thank their many friends and neighbors for their actions and expressions of support. The only negative remarks were those Clementine heard from her own parents, who stopped by on Thursday to complain about how they were the last ones to hear of their grandson's kidnapping, and how they felt like they had been ignored all summer. Fortunately Flea arrived soon after the Goodens and silenced them with the announcement that Clementine had again dominated the baked-sweets category of the BIF Culinary Competition. "You got a blue ribbon for your apple pie, and a red one for your cherry."

"How much more American can you get!" Henry cheered. He was feeling mighty wibberniffled. He could hardly wait for Pat and Talbert Gooden and the rest of the guests to leave.

It would be unfair to say that Holly was not relieved to have Archibald home—of course she was—but her emotions were focused on the upcoming weekend. She avoided the celebratory fuss surrounding her now-famous brother and began an hour-by-hour countdown to parade time. Mindful of her new modesty, she did not count aloud. Indeed, she was practically withdrawn. Even when Warren professed that he certainly had enjoyed participating in the kissing custom, her reply to him was cool. "Traditions are made to uphold," she said, then walked to the barn to give Dan a rubdown.

Emmet, having grown up with Archibald, had assumed all along that his brother was indestructible. So when the episode was over and Archibald safely home, Emmet was relieved for the sake of his parents. He was also relieved because he knew he would be free to roam in Binkerton on Saturday and, if all went well, free to court Contessa. Senator, ever the good soldier, was relieved because Emmet was relieved.

Matilda was so relieved at her brother's safe return, she accidentally broke her vow of silence and told Leopold, "Thank the powers that be! Now that Archibald is safe, I don't care if Dad tans my hide blue. I deserve a thousand lashes, at least."

"You should be strung up by your pigtails and left to dangle for a week," Leopold teased. "Yet at the same time you deserve congratulations. You traced an invisible thread to the source of a secret. That takes talent, Matilda. And you flew. You flew a carpet! I'm more than seven times your age, and I've never known anyone to perform a more amazing feat."

"I admit it was pretty amazing," she allowed. "Except I almost got my little brother killed."

"That wasn't your doing. You're not responsible for that."

"Indirectly I am. But thanks for forgiving me. Now I have to face Mom and Dad . . . and Aunt Emma. When she learns what happened, she'll disown me as a niece. I'm so ashamed."

"Ah," Leopold cleared his throat. "I could speak with her on your behalf. Maybe temper her wrath a bit."

"Would you?"

"I'll try, yes. In the meantime we'll keep the flight a secret. I've already spoken with Archibald. He understands."

"You mean Dad didn't find out about it?" Matilda's voice cracked with disbelief.

"Not as far as I'm aware. I haven't told him. Of course no one believes Crowley. And the two nephews agreed with me that it would be wise for them to keep quiet. By the way, they aren't bad kids. They just never had a chance to do good. Garland and I dis-

cussed it, and he's going to try to hire them to work at his place . . .
maybe keep them from going to jail."

Matilda looked hopefully at Leopold. "So, what you're saying is
that no one really knows besides us?"

"You, me, Holly, and Archibald."

From the moment of his triumphant return, Archibald received
such a steady outpouring of cheer and goodwill, he began to wonder
if the Pope in Rome was jealous. Honor was added to his joy when a
hand-delivered letter arrived on the farm. Addressed to Master
Archibald Dither, it was written on the red-and-gold stationery of
the Binkerton Volunteer Fire Department. It said: "So that everyone
may have the opportunity to congratulate you on the felicitous outcome of your ordeal, you are invited to ride on the mayor's float in
the parade on Saturday. If you choose to accept, please be present in
the main pavilion at ten A.M. on July 4th. You are welcome to invite
one family member or friend to accompany you." The letter was
signed by Eugenna White. Archibald wasted no time selecting a
friend. "I want Carl with me on the mayor's float."

On Friday night Leopold sat at home in his Inner Sanctum. It had
been an intense week. He had hoped to have a little time to spend
with Emma Bean, but on Wednesday Emma had accepted an invitation from Flea to join her for a few days at a spa in the Blue Ridge
Mountains. "So it goes sometimes," he muttered to himself as he
poured a shot of eau-de-vie and leaned back in his easy chair. He
propped his feet on the worktable, gazed up at the flap-wing flying
machine, and chuckled. His mood was mixed. He was amused and
relieved by the recent run of events, but at the same time he was a
little sad. Earlier in the week he had been in the fray of humanity,
playing a critical role in the protection of that all-important duo-
concept, *liberty* and *life*, but now the matter was resolved and he no
longer felt needed. He sensed that time was returning to its abun-

dant state, and he would soon have more of it than he needed or could use. With a gulp he swallowed the eau-de-vie. As the clear liquid warmed his insides, he glanced at the fragments of manuscript littering his worktable. Just looking at the piles of paper made him weary. *"The Comprehensive Guide,"* he laughed aloud. "The useless product of an abstract mind." The dark thought that he might never finish the book flitted across his consciousness. He shuddered at the notion, then poured another shot of eau-de-vie. "Those tattered sheets are you, old man. That's right . . . you . . . me . . . . us. All I got. A lifetime of nights inked out alone in this room we call our Inner Sanctum. It's your gilded cup, and guess what—it won't even hold water." Leopold lifted the glass and drank again. His innards warmed another degree. "Watch it now, Leopold, you're starting to talk to yourself. Who cares? I do. Who? Me? No, you. Heehee. Okay, one more weeny splash. Don't mind if I do. You don't, do you? Hehehee."

Alice and Jimmy Aylor hosted a dinner that same Friday night for Bellamonte Smoot, Millie Ross, Missy Hobkins, Garland Barlow, Wade Butcher, Flugga Gibson, and Buddy Breedon. John Washington and Felton Fibbs had been invited, but they opted to celebrate at the Hot Spot, where there had been many offers to stand them for drinks. Carl Plummers was also invited, but he declined. He was saving his energy for the parade. For the first time in many years, he intended to leave the store. Arrangements had already been made for several men and a truck to pick him up and haul him to Binkerton.

At Dither Farm, as if there wasn't already enough happiness in the air, Clementine gathered the whole family in the kitchen to make an important announcement. "Your father and I have discussed the matter with Aunt Emma, and she agrees that it would be the best thing for everyone if . . ." Clementine took a breath and patted her rounded belly. "Well, Henry and I have always felt that six would be the perfect number for children. And we decided we'd like to adopt Warren. That is," she addressed the visitor from New Hampshire, "if you think you'd like to live with us." The room was silent for a moment while Warren looked at the floor and absorbed the news.

"You should do what you want, son," advised Henry. "You know you're welcome here."

Warren continued gazing at his feet, then raised his head and calmly met the eyes of each of the Dithers in turn. The smile that slowly spread across Warren's face prompted the family to cheer and rush to smother him with hugs. "I reckon I'm not a Yankee Doodle Dandy any longer!" he said.

Saturday, July the Fourth, finally arrived. Holly wondered if she was still dreaming, or if there really were only two minutes to go before noon. She could feel Dan's excitement. They stood six inches from a canvas curtain erected at the beginning of Lacy Lane. She leaned forward to scratch his ear and whisper, "Dan, you are the most handsome beast in the world. Let's show this crowd what style is all about." Behind her, Holly could hear the murmur of anxious voices mixing with the squeaks of nervous instruments. Off to the side she heard Warren call.

"A hundred seconds," he said.

A hundred years, Holly thought. That was the length of time she intended to spend with him. "Thanks." Holly blew him a kiss and was pleased to note that it landed on a proud, smiling face.

Suddenly Eugenna White popped through an opening in the curtain with her clipboard held aloft. She looked at Holly, nodded, blew a plastic whistle, then dropped her arm. It was the signal for the parade to begin. *Boom* went a bass drum. *Ah-ooga* went an antique-car horn. The curtain was pulled away. Holly hesitated for one second, then nudged Dan into a high-stepping prance. They were greeted by a roar of wild cheers rising from a sea of faces and flags. Holly squared her shoulders and smiled modestly at the masses. She tipped her silver-sequined cowgirl hat. This is not a dream, she told herself.

Following her down Lacy Lane were one hundred and nine separate entries, including two marching bands, three teams of baton-twirling majorettes, rescue and fire-fighting squads, civic functionaries in convertibles, kids on bicycles decorated with red, white, and blue streamers, antique cars, tractors pulling floats, uniformed war veterans, and the recently crowned Princess of the Binkerton Independence Festival. Lining the sidewalks a dozen deep, there were over five thousand people in attendance. Holly sprang into a standing position on Dan's back and waved. She was rewarded with an explosion of clicking cameras and spirited applause. Her heart fluttered wildly, and it was all she could do to concentrate on keeping her balance.

Flea, who had returned from the spa that morning, was having a hard time seeing through the crowd, so she pushed forward to where children and short people lined the curb. She was feeling chipper as she found a clear spot and sat down to wait for the parade. Her thoughts were with Holly, whom she could see in the distance, when suddenly someone's breath tickled the back of her neck. Then a deep voice whispered in her ear, "That sure is a fetching outfit, Flea."

Flea turned slowly. "Garland. Have you been drinking?"

"No, indeed. Not a drop." Garland squatted so that he was at eye level with Flea.

"Then what's got into you, acting like this?"

"That, I can't really say. Maybe I've had too much excitement this summer. Whatever . . ." Garland shrugged shyly. "I just thought I'd come over and pitch a woo."

Flea turned a peppery red. "I agree with you; there has been plenty of excitement lately."

211

"Too much." Garland sat on the curb. As he did, his hand accidentally touched Flea's. She did not pull away.

Whether it was because he had slept so well the night before, or because it just happened to be a beautiful day, Leopold, for the first time in more than a dozen years, came down off his hill and attended the BIF Fourth of July Parade. He was still a little fuzzy from his eau-de-vie binge, so he avoided the press of the crowd and sat on the back of a bench in the town park. From there he could get the flavor of the parade without having his feathers ruffled.

Emmet spotted Leopold sitting on the bench. He turned to Contessa and took her hand. "Come on. I want to introduce you to the man who gave me my monkey. People say he's an eccentric, but I don't hold it against him."

As the young couple approached Leopold, he could see that Emmet wanted to create a serious impression. He stepped down from the bench and waited. When they reached the bench and stopped, Leopold bowed politely.

Emmet smiled. "Contessa, this is Mr. Hillacre. We call him Leopold. Leopold, this is Contessa."

"I am pleased to meet you," said Leopold, shaking the girl's small hand.

"As am I," Contessa replied with a curtsey.

"He collects more stuff than me and Senator," Emmet said.

"Speaking of Senator, where is he?" asked Leopold.

A grin jumped from Contessa's face to Emmet's. "The last we saw him, he was in the pavilion with Rosey."

"That's my father's monkey. She's a girl," added Contessa.

"Oh, what kind?" asked Leopold.

"She's a macaque, from the East Indies."

"She's a few years older than Senator," said Emmet. "But he doesn't seem to notice."

"Well, well." Leopold rubbed his chin and chuckled.

The front of the parade passed the corner of the park, and they could hear the musical strains of the Hunkerdowns. They filled the air with a bluegrass version of "I've Got to Be Me."

"We should go now," said Emmet.

"Nice to meet you," said Contessa.

"Been a pleasure," mumbled Leopold.

Leopold watched Emmet and Contessa depart hand in hand. As they disappeared into the crowd, he noticed a flash of red running toward the park. It was Matilda. She ran to within forty yards of the bench and hollered, "Good. I found you. Wait there. Don't go away."

While Leopold waited, the mayor's float slowly approached the packed intersection of Lacy Lane and Elm Street. This was the focal point of the parade. Clementine and Henry had been waiting there for hours. The mayor's float was a sparse, elegant affair, little more than a hay wagon dressed up in red, white, and blue paper. At the front of the wagon, near where the hitch joined the tractor, stood a maypole decorated with streamers and colorful balloons. Around the outer edge of the float were bouquets of wildflowers, which were connected by a chain of daisies. A bench and two chairs were set in the center of the wagon. Carl (because of balance, not rank) occupied the bench in the middle. He wore blue overalls, a white shirt, and a red bow tie. Many in the crowd saluted and called to him. He lifted a chubby hand and waved to one and all. It was apparent from his smile that he was one of the happiest men in the world. To his left was the mayor of Binkerton, Harlow Wickerbee. He wore a black-and-white tuxedo. On Carl's right, nattily attired in his Sunday best, sat the young celebrity from Aylor's Store. As the float neared the intersection, Clementine jumped and shouted with excitement, "Here they come! I hope he sees us."

At that instant Archibald stood and surveyed the crowd for his mother and father. When he saw them, he moved to the edge of the float. A happy tear slid down Clementine's cheek as Archibald bowed and court-rolled his right arm. The crowd roared with approval. Archibald was inspired by the moment. He turned, winked at his buddy Carl, then did something that was remembered in Binkerton for many, many years to come. He threw off his jacket, kicked off his shoes, loosened his tie, wiggled his ears, wobbled his elbows, and began a command performance of the chicken dance.

Laughter erupted in the streets and passed contagiously from person to person, until even those who could not see the dance were chuckling. Within minutes it was mass hysterics. No one could get hold of themselves. And the longer the laughing lasted, the more intense it became. Soon, from the tip of Dan's nose at the front of the parade to the rear of the pavilion where Senator and Rosey jabbered gaily, the town of Binkerton was expressing itself in a giant peal of merriment. Even the Princess got a bellyache from laughing so hard. She fell to her knees and begged for Archibald to please stop doing the chicken dance.

Leopold remained on the bench in the small park and listened to the outbreak of mirth rising around him. He could not see Archibald. It occurred to him that the world had finally gone mad. Or, rather, gone happy. He could understand that; he had nearly done so just the night before. He made a mental note of a premise he intended to develop and include in *The Comprehensive Guide*: Laughter released on earth ascends into heaven and tickles the bottoms of angels' feet.

His thoughts were interrupted by a woman's voice. "Leopold," it said. He recognized it immediately. It was the voice that had spoken to him under the tree that night at Aylor's Store. He turned and was startled to see Emma Bean standing in the park.

"Music to the ears," Emma said.

"Yes. A very happy crowd." Leopold stood. "How are you? I didn't expect to see you here."

"I'm just fine." Emma beamed as she sat on the bench. She indicated with a gesture for Leopold to join her. When he did, he detected the smell of cinnamon. "So. Matilda tells me numerous unusual events took place while I was in Washington."

"Yes. They were numerous and unusual."

"Matilda is such a sweetheart. I've invited her to visit my home in Iceland later this summer. August is the best time of year up there. She'll need a chaperon, of course."

"Is, ah," Leopold cleared his throat, "that an invitation?"

"She claims you are the only one who can fill me in on the details of what happened here." Emma's white teeth flashed in the sunlight when she smiled. "You could fly up."

"Fly? Why, yes. I suppose we could." Leopold felt like turning a cartwheel.

Emma reached and touched his hand. "Perhaps we have time now for me to see your butterfly collection."

"Time? You bet we do. There's plenty of that." Leopold took Emma's hand in his and stood. "Come, Miss Bean. I will take you to my Inner Sanctum."